It started when I dropped a pen and got down on my knees to search for it—only to discover that Rob was down there, too.

"Hi, stranger," he said, staring at me.

"Uh, hi." My fingers had found the pen. But the rest of me stayed where it was.

Rob came a little closer. "Hey," he whispered, "this could be, like, a fresh beginning for us." He grabbed for the pen; or my hand, I couldn't tell which. But it didn't matter—because his face had found mine and was moving in.

Bantam Sweet Dreams Romances
Ask your bookseller for the books you have missed

#1 P.S. I LOVE YOU
#2 THE POPULARITY PLAN
#3 LAURIE'S SONG
#4 PRINCESS AMY
#5 LITTLE SISTER
#6 CALIFORNIA GIRL
#7 GREEN EYES
#8 THE THOROUGHBRED
#9 COVER GIRL
#10 LOVE MATCH
#11 THE PROBLEM WITH LOVE
#12 NIGHT OF THE PROM
#13 THE SUMMER JENNY FELL
    IN LOVE
#14 DANCE OF LOVE
#15 THINKING OF YOU
#16 HOW DO YOU SAY GOODBYE
#17 ASK ANNIE
#18 TEN-BOY SUMMER
#19 LOVE SONG
#20 THE POPULARITY SUMMER
#21 ALL'S FAIR IN LOVE
#22 SECRET IDENTITY
#23 FALLING IN LOVE AGAIN
#24 THE TROUBLE WITH
    CHARLIE
#25 HER SECRET SELF
#26 IT MUST BE MAGIC
#27 TOO YOUNG FOR LOVE
#28 TRUSTING HEARTS
#29 NEVER LOVE A COWBOY
#30 LITTLE WHITE LIES
#31 TOO CLOSE FOR COMFORT
#32 DAYDREAMER
#33 DEAR AMANDA
#34 COUNTRY GIRL
#35 FORBIDDEN LOVE
#36 SUMMER DREAMS
#37 PORTRAIT OF LOVE
#38 RUNNING MATES
#39 FIRST LOVE

#40 SECRETS
#41 THE TRUTH ABOUT ME &
    BOBBY V.
#42 THE PERFECT MATCH
#43 TENDER LOVING CARE
#44 LONG DISTANCE LOVE
#45 DREAM PROM
#46 ON THIN ICE
#47 TE AMO MEANS I LOVE YOU
#48 DIAL L FOR LOVE
#49 TOO MUCH TO LOSE
#50 LIGHTS, CAMERA, LOVE
#51 MAGIC MOMENTS
#52 LOVE NOTES
#53 GHOST OF A CHANCE
#54 I CAN'T FORGET YOU
#55 SPOTLIGHT ON LOVE
#56 CAMPFIRE NIGHTS
#57 ON HER OWN
#58 RHYTHM OF LOVE
#59 PLEASE SAY YES
#60 SUMMER BREEZES
#61 EXCHANGE OF HEARTS
#62 JUST LIKE THE MOVIES
#63 KISS ME, CREEP
#64 LOVE IN THE FAST LANE
#65 THE TWO OF US
#66 LOVE TIMES TWO
#67 I BELIEVE IN YOU
#68 LOVEBIRDS
#69 CALL ME BEAUTIFUL
#70 SPECIAL SOMEONE
#71 TOO MANY BOYS
#72 GOODBYE FOREVER
#73 LANGUAGE OF LOVE
#74 DON'T FORGET ME
#75 FIRST SUMMER LOVE
#76 THREE CHEERS FOR LOVE
#77 TEN-SPEED SUMMER
#78 NEVER SAY NO

Never Say No

Jean Capron

BANTAM BOOKS

TORONTO • NEW YORK • LONDON • SYDNEY • AUCKLAND

RL 6, IL age 11 and up

NEVER SAY NO
A Bantam Book / January 1985

Cover photo by Pat Hill.

ISBN 0-553-24384-5

Published simultaneously in the United States and Canada

PRINTED IN THE UNITED STATES OF AMERICA

O   0 9 8 7 6 5 4 3 2 1

Never Say No

Chapter One

That October Mr. Baldwin, our visual arts teacher, assigned Rob Carney to another seat, one in the corner, over by the windows. Away from me at last.

All right, I'll admit it, I did complain to Mr. Baldwin. And why not? After years of Rob breathing down my neck in every class we'd suffered through together, I'd had it.

At first Mr. Baldwin was hesitant to change Rob's seat; he thought he had a better solution for handling our personality conflict. "Rob seems perfectly content where he is," he told me. "You're the one who's objecting, Betsy, so why don't I leave Rob there and move you? That should work out just fine."

"You're the teacher," I said. "But you don't know Rob Carney the way I do. He'll find a way to follow me."

And sure enough. I moved, and Rob found someone to switch seats with so that he was sitting near me again.

Mr. Baldwin finally saw the light. He gave Rob the corner seat and made it permanent.

Life was going to be simpler and pleasanter with my best friend, Sandy James, sitting behind me—although I could have been happier without her chatter about Rob. "The poor guy looks lonesome," she whispered in my left ear.

"Tough," I muttered, rearranging my pen-and-ink supplies and opening up the visual arts manual.

"So you could have ignored him," she said. "I'm sure he doesn't mean to cause you pain and agony. Besides," she added, "maybe you should feel flattered by the attention. He *is* kind of cute."

Flattered? Forget it. And "cute" was a term that Rob Carney would never fit in a million years. He's long and skinny, with a good-sized nose charitably described as "interesting," piercing blue eyes, and a mop of brown hair crying for emergency combing.

To me, "cute" was Josh Amberston, who sat up front by the door. Tall, well filled out, with copper-colored curls, brooding dark eyes, and a strong jaw. Josh is the kind of guy who could put on somebody's old, patched throwaways and come out looking like a doll. Whereas, no matter what he wore, Rob would always manage to look as if he had on third generation hand-me-downs.

"Rob's drawing you again," Sandy whispered. "He keeps glancing over here, then making these squiggles in his sketch pad. Another Rob Carney original. Talk about obsessions."

Rob had been doing that since the third grade when he drew my head as a lopsided circle with corkscrew curls, crayoned dots for eyes, and a half-moon mouth. I will say that with the years his skills had improved. I only hoped that Rob might redirect his artistic focus to something or someone else.

We'd been working on cartoons for a month in class, mostly studying the history of them, such as that comics had started back in the 1890s with strips called "The Yellow Kid" and "Katzenjammer Kids" and "Happy Hooligan." We had worked on some of the simpler mechanics. We'd learned to select idea sketches and pencil them onto typing paper, block out figures, and then letter in the dialogue and surround it with a "balloon." Once we had some of the basics down, we tried drawing in ink. We were about to embark on the main project for the semester: cartoon series or comic strips of our own.

Mr. Baldwin was really big on cartooning. He called it a "distinctive art form." According to him some cartoons are now being exhibited in the Louvre Museum in Paris and the Smithsonian Institution in Washington, D.C. He wanted each project to be shared by two people—an idea person paired with an artist, both sharing the work and the glory. And because I'm basically an idea person—who can also fill in with the final inking and other drudgery—my fate was sealed.

I glanced around, mentally ticking off the artists in our group. Eventually my gaze settled on Josh Amberston. With his shirt unbuttoned to the middle of his chest and his sleeves rolled up to just below his elbows—doing great things for his forearms—he was worth looking at. Besides, he could put together a pretty good strip. Oh, maybe not so good as—some people. I sneaked a glance toward the corner of the room. But so what? We were all amateurs, just learning. Anyway, I'd pretty much decided on sharing the burden with Josh. So it was a little unsettling to hear the first pairing.

"Sandy James and Josh Amberston will work together." Straight from Mr. Baldwin's mouth.

I turned and caught the stunned expression on Sandy's round face. She'd hit the jackpot, all right. It would take awhile for her to come down.

A buzz of voices took over as everyone looked around and tried to figure out who he or she would be paired with. Except me. As I had explained to Sandy earlier, if Josh was out, I really couldn't care less whom Mr. Baldwin matched me with. After all, it was just a project. Six weeks of sharing classroom chores with another human being and getting graded for it. No big deal.

Mr. Baldwin rapped on his desk with a ruler. "Settle down, folks, and let me con-

5

tinue. The following students will share their talents.

"Joe Ansara and Michelle Blaine."

Good choice. Besides which, they adored each other.

"Bill Goldbloom and Mike Hennessey."

A perfect blending of brains and talent. So far, top combinations.

"Rob Carney and Betsy Marsh."

I sat up straight. "Hey—"

"Wendy Abel and Jeanette Brill."

"Wait!"

Mr. Baldwin's voice droned on, washing mine out.

"Take heart, friend," Sandy murmured behind me. "It's just a project, remember? Six weeks of sharing chores. No big deal."

I could hear her snicker. Some joke. Well, we'd see who had the last laugh.

I aimed a glare at the corner chair in the row by the windows. Rob had slouched low in his seat and was thumbing through his manual, managing to avoid my eye. But there was a hint of a smile on his lips.

I approached Mr. Baldwin's desk, fully prepared to lay it on the line. "Later, Betsy," he said as he waved me away. "All the teams are to get together at three o'clock in the second-floor study hall. If you have something to say, you'll get your chance then."

All right, I'd wait until then.

I got to the study hall a little late. The other kids were already grouped in twos around the library tables, with their spiral notebooks opened and pens poised—except for Rob, who sat by himself, next to an empty chair. Was he saving it for me? Because if he was—

"Hi, Betsy," he said. And he gave me this wide grin. "Been waiting."

"Betsy," Mr. Baldwin called out, "will you please sit down next to Rob? I'd like to get on with the business at hand."

I sat down.

Mr. Baldwin launched into the ground rules. It seemed we could make some choices about our projects, if not our partners. We could choose to do either political cartoons, single gag cartoons, or adventure or comic strips with continuing characters and situations. Those of us selecting continuing strips were to complete five black-and-whites with three panels each and one twelve-paneled

Sunday-type strip in color. We idea people would be graded on the sharpness of our story lines or the humor of our jokes. And the cartoonists would be graded on their originality and drawing skills.

Beside me, Rob was fumbling with his sketch pad, inching it open to a blank page. From the corner of my eye, I watched him pencil in Mr. Baldwin's features and, with swift, sure finger movements, etch an eyebrow, form the mouth and the familiar mustache. He'd just begun the hairline when—

"Rob Carney," Mr. Baldwin's deep voice filled the room, "are we to assume you have a sample of your art to show us?"

"Uh, just a rough sketch." Looking faintly uncomfortable, Rob slid his pad to his knees. "Nothing worth advertising."

But it was. He'd captured Mr. Baldwin's looks with those few bold strokes. In spite of myself I was impressed. Not with the guy. Just with his artistic skills.

Mr. Baldwin gave us bits of advice about how to fit the ideas or gags to the cartoon characters and said a few words about the proper pens, paper, inks, and other technical stuff. Then he entertained us with humorous examples of how *real* cartoonists coped in their mad, mad world.

In the meantime Rob had reopened the sketch pad on his lap and was doodling like crazy. I grabbed a quick peek. This spindly little guy stared back. Hollowed eyes in a gaunt, whiskered face. Flappy ears. Tufts of hair sticking out from under a battered sombrero. Suspenders draped over a small potbelly. Huge, clownlike shoes.

"You like?" Rob whispered softly.

"Not bad," I had to admit. But that was all I would admit. For instance, he'd never hear from me that something about his spindly creature had touched me. Was it those ridiculous ears, barely holding up the ancient sombrero? Or, was it the eyes?

Mr. Baldwin was summing up. "You can work out your problems in the classroom, at home, in the study halls, wherever you can find a quiet spot. It's not important where, or even the exact steps you go through to get to your goal. What I'm asking, at this stage, is that two weeks from today you deliver—in rough-draft form—your concept of an acceptable cartoon or strip."

I sat quietly and looked at my notes. I

heard Rob say, "Well?" I favored him with a frosty glance, then looked away.

Josh and Sandy were *really* consulting. I mean, heads together, voices pitched, both sounding agreeable. "Personally," Josh said, his voice rising, "I'd like to go for the strips. What's your input, Sandy?"

"If that's what you want," Sandy sang back, her cheeks pink, her big blue eyes shining, "it's fine with me."

Sandy, how could you? I thought.

"Now there's what every guy here can appreciate," Rob commented to the air. "A cooperative partner."

"Hey, did I ask to be your partner?" I didn't give him a chance to respond. "We both know the answer to that one, don't we? Carney, I'll tell you this just once—"

A number of heads swiveled in our direction. Including the teacher's. It seemed smarter to stop or rather to postpone it.

"I realize," Mr. Baldwin said, "not every team will be perfectly matched. There will be sharp differences of opinion, even bursts of temperament. So be it. I strongly suspect that by the time these six weeks are over, several of you will have learned much more about getting along with your partner than you will about putting together a comic strip."

Most of the kids had gathered up their stuff and were heading for the exit. Only Rob and I lagged behind. He had his reasons, I had mine.

Rob put his hand on my arm. "Betsy—"

I pulled my arm away.

He winced as if I'd struck him. Then he took a long breath. "OK," he said, "have it your way. Go over there to Mr. Baldwin and tell him you want out. I'm sure it can be arranged." He scooped up his sketch pad, papers, and books from the table. "I don't care. Doesn't bother me one little bit." Then he stuffed the papers inside his visual arts manual.

One white sheet drifted away from the others and fluttered to my feet, where it lay, looking pathetic.

The least I could do was pick it up.

I glanced at the paper, and, of course, there he was—the little guy again.

I wonder what would have happened if I'd had sense enough to let it go at that, if I'd simply turned the scribbling over to Rob, spoken my piece to Mr. Baldwin, and gone on my way.

But something about that gaunt, penciled figure held me. Was it the clunky old shoes? The funny ears? Who knows what?

Mr. Baldwin caught sight of me. "Ah, yes, Betsy," he said, remembering at last. "You wanted to talk to me?"

My eyes brushed past Rob, then returned, staying on that familiar face for a bare instant. I saw him draw in another long breath. I looked away. "Uh, no, Mr. Baldwin," I said. "Not really. I was just waiting for—for my partner here to get his act together."

I walked to the door and turned to Rob. "Well?" I gave him my cool stare. "Are you coming or not?"

Sometimes I don't understand myself at all.

Chapter Two

The walk home seemed to take forever. Rob hung close to my heels, spouting enthusiastic messages about what great partners we'd make and mentioning that he had lots of ideas about what we'd do with the funny little character.

"Ideas?" I said icily. "Maybe we should get this straight here and now, Carney. I'm supposed to be the idea person, you're supposed to be the cartoonist. Remember?"

"Well, yeah. But . . ." The corners of his mouth turned down, and he looked away from me.

"Of course," I added grudgingly, "there probably will have to be some give-and-take. I

13

mean, if it happens that your idea is so appealing—so absolutely right for the character—"

"Exactly." He grinned. "Just what I had in mind. And if you want to lend a hand with my creation, maybe sketch in a line or two—feel free."

His creation? Hmmm.

I didn't invite Rob in. But then, I never had. Over the years our prickly relationship had always been conducted somewhere else: in the school playground and other kids' backyards when we were younger; and in classes, corridors, the school gym, the cafeteria, and downtown fast-food spots by the time we'd made it to our present ages of sixteen. It seemed that he was always showing up wherever I was. For a while he'd call on the phone, asking for me in what he'd assumed was a totally disguised voice. I'd trained my family to tell him I'd just left the house and wouldn't be back for hours. The calls had dwindled to maybe one a month. We could all live with that.

"Who was that you were talking to?" my mother asked, tearing herself away from the front window.

"Uh—"

"It looked very much like that Carney boy, to me," she surmised. "But I seriously doubt you would—"

"Oh, it's Rob, all right." I made a face.

"Well, if he's still bothering you, I'll call his mother. She's a reasonable woman, we get along well, I could suggest—"

"No!"

It seemed a good idea to spell out the whole thing—the cartoon project, the necessary teamwork, the pairing up with Rob, and that it would last a mere six weeks. "I'll survive it somehow," I announced airily.

"Fine," she said. "Let's hope the rest of us can."

So the family wasn't exactly crazy about Rob. I guess that could be blamed on me. I'd said plenty about him over the years and none of it was complimentary.

That evening we were seated around the dinner table, my little brother, Teddy, to my right, my older sister, Joanne, across the way, Dad and Mom in their usual places. I was putting away a generous helping of spaghetti and meatballs when the phone rang.

Joanne, who was expecting a long distance call, got to it first. "Betsy?" she echoed. She glanced over at me and winked. "Gosh, Rob, I'm sorry, you just missed her. She won't be back until at least ten—"

I'd already pushed back my chair. "I'm here," I said.

"That's a new one," Joanne murmured, handing me the receiver.

"I'm going to speak to Mr. Baldwin," Rob's voice came across the line, "about reserving that reading room off the magazine room for us tomorrow after school."

"The reading room? But it's so *small*." Just barely enough room for Rob and me, and maybe one other person, if you squeezed us all in tight. I simply could not see myself holed up in that tiny space with Rob Carney for even one afternoon.

"Or," he said less cheerfully, "I suppose we could use the magazine library. Hardly anybody uses it. And it is roomier—if you go in for roomy."

"I do," I said. "Put me down for the magazine library."

"But—"

Enough. "See you, Carney." And I hung up loudly.

"You tell him, kid," Joanne said, returning to her spaghetti.

"Don't let the boy con you into anything you don't want to do, baby," Dad contributed, reaching for a dinner roll. "The butter, please."

Mom nodded and smiled and handed Dad the butter plate, and Teddy slurped several strands of spaghetti, signaling that the conversation was over.

So much for Rob Carney and his little reading room.

It turned out that the reading room was quickly snatched up by two people who didn't seem to mind the lack of space. Sandy and Josh had squeezed themselves into it and were perfectly at home.

"Like they say," I muttered from behind my hand, "it takes all kinds."

"You had your chance," Rob said. He sneaked a look into the partly opened door, eased his head back, and glanced over at me. "Just think. That could be us."

Or me—and Josh.

Rob and I sat across from each other at the long library table in the magazine room. I opened the visual arts textbook and tried to concentrate on it, flipping pages every now and then to show I meant business. But Rob's under-the-breath humming and his finger-tips clacking out a beat against the varnished oak table made it impossible to concentrate. Oh, it was going to be a *great* six weeks.

"Carney," I said finally, "will you kindly refrain from making those annoying sounds?"

His fingertips stopped in midair. "Gosh," he answered, "can't a guy even relax without your making a big deal out of it?"

"Relax? You call it relaxing to thump and hum? And you have some nerve to sit there and look hurt while I make a perfectly justified request."

Rob sat up straight. "Now just a minute! Speaking of *justified*—"

"Well, well, Betsy and Rob!" Mr. Baldwin's voice carried in from the doorway. "I see you're already seated, wide awake, and ready for action."

Twin mumbles, from our side of the room.

Mr. Baldwin approached the oak table where we were sitting, and pulled up a chair. "Glad you could work after school. Do either of you have preliminary sketches, or even a vague idea of what your strip will be about?"

Rob hesitated, glanced furtively my way, then hauled out a mess of papers from the battered accordian-pleated folder he'd brought with him.

The little guy. Of course.

Mr. Baldwin scanned the sketches quickly, then went back over them, one by one. He scribbled some notes in a spiral tablet and straightened Rob's papers into a neat pile. "You've got the beginnings of something there," he said. "Something pretty special, if you handle it right."

After Mr. Baldwin left Rob spread out some of the best sketches and frowned at them. "What did he mean, handle it right?"

I shrugged.

It seemed smarter to turn our thoughts to something else, and we decided to christen our guy with a name. There was a drawn-out pause. "I see a—*W*," I finally said. "Yeah, he's definitely a *W*. Willie." I tested it on my tongue. "Walter. Winston." Not yet.

"Let's dig into what we've got here," Rob said. "Scrawny little fella with flappy ears.

Looks like a stiff breeze would send him flying—"

"Stiff breeze," I repeated after him. Then, "That's a small wind. Wind begins with *W*. Windy," I came up with in triumph. "That's his name!"

Rob smiled. It was catching; I actually smiled back.

We started to find a last name. Something that wouldn't clash with Windy. "I got the idea for that face from my mom's uncle, who lives in New Hampshire," Rob said. "He's a strange little character, with an even stranger wife. And the summer we went to Walpole to visit them—"

"Walpole?"

"Right. Walpole, New Hampshire." He stared at me. "Hey! Do we have a name?" He stood up and glanced about, as if searching out applause. All he got from me was a brief nod.

Windy Walpole. I guess we could have done worse.

We had until four o'clock when Mrs. Benton, who's in charge of locking up the second-floor rooms, chases everyone out. We made the best of our time.

We decided that Windy would be a sort of scruffy loser, with a sharp-tongued wife—whom Rob sketched with rapid strokes, bringing forth an odd-shaped, pointy-faced person. After a spirited discussion, we came up with her name: Hannah. And then we batted around some more ideas. For instance, should the Walpoles have children? We settled on a teenage daughter, Rosalie.

Rob began penciling in a ridiculous-looking girl who had inherited the most laughable features of both her parents.

"Hold it," I said. "How about making her a beauty instead? As if the Walpoles' genes had accidentally cranked out this gorgeous winner, and neither of them knows how to handle it. I'll bet we can get plenty of mileage from that twist. In fact, I think—"

Rob's pencil was already grazing the paper. Quickly he drew a delicately boned creature. The face was a squared-off oval, the eyes, large and thick-lashed. His Rosalie had a fawnlike quality, as if one quick movement would send her scurrying into the forest.

"Not bad," I conceded. "If you go for the shy but gorgeous type."

"My specialty," Rob said. He opened his mouth as if about to say something else.

"In five minutes everybody scoot," Mrs. Benton's ready soprano rang out.

Rob and I jumped up at the same time, bumping into each other. We stared into each other's eyes. I looked away first.

A small silence, then, "Hey," he said softly, "we work pretty well together, know that?" He moved forward, a tiny smile playing on his lips.

He was standing much closer to me than I usually allowed. I considered edging away, but then I thought, *Why should I?* I looked up, directing an extremely cool gaze at him, and kept it there, needing to make him back down. He seemed not the least bit ruffled—if anything, he was calmer and steadier than usual.

We might have stood there until Christmas, with our eyes locked, if the reading room door hadn't sprung open.

Josh and Sandy came out of the tiny room together, obviously more chummy than when they had gone in. And they were bursting with enthusiasm about their project. "It's going to be an adventure strip," Josh announced. "A

22

sort of updated 'Dick Tracy.' We decided to name the hero—"

"Bo McClure," Sandy finished for him. "And Bo's love will be a mysterious, dark-haired stranger who's just moved to town. She's occupying a spooky old mansion on the outskirts—"

"And they'll meet on a dark and stormy night—maybe on Halloween, we're not sure yet—"

"We," I cut in, "are creating a comic strip. And our characters are pretty cute, if I do have to say so myself."

Beside me, Rob shifted from one foot to the other.

"Not only that," I added, "we have actual sketches. Care to see them?"

But Mrs. Benton, jangling her many keys, would have none of it. "I said *five minutes*. And that didn't mean six."

Josh and Sandy hurried down the hall, talking rapid fire about their strips. I grabbed my stuff and tried to catch up to them, leaving Rob behind.

But Josh and Sandy were too fast. I saw them running out the front door of the school. When I got outside, I paused on the top of the stairs. Something had gone wrong with our afternoon weather. What had started out as a crisp but sunny fall day had disintegrated into the sort of cold drizzle that is typical of October. I drew my sweater about me and watched, shivering a little, as Josh and Sandy hurried down the street, shoulder to shoulder.

It wouldn't have killed Josh to walk us both home. He didn't live all that far from me—just a couple of streets over. Sandy probably wouldn't care if we dropped her off, then made it through the rain to my house. Or would she?

So I'd walk home alone. No catastrophe.

Somebody's fingers attached themselves to my elbow. "Walk you home?" Rob's voice came through gruffly.

I like to think I didn't outwardly jump. "Rob Carney," I said, gritting my teeth, "haven't you ever heard of barking before you bite?"

He shrugged and smiled. "Sorry. All I wanted to know was—"

"Can you walk me home." My lips came together in a tight line. "Thanks, but no thanks."

The smile faded. "OK, if that's the way you

want it. But don't say I didn't ask." He turned abruptly and stomped down Summerfield High's front steps.

I could see him pause at the corner, then take a sharp left and head for Locust Avenue. He was moving right along, each step quicker than the one before. In a few minutes I couldn't see him at all.

The evening's dinner fare was meat loaf, scalloped potatoes, and my mother's special salad, topped off with lemon chiffon pie. All my favorites.

"Something wrong with the meat loaf?" Mom questioned. "And you've never passed up the scalloped potatoes before. What's going on here?"

"Nothing," I said. "Everything's fine, as always. I'm just not hungry."

"Then you must be coming down with something."

Well, I did have a sort of knotted feeling at the pit of my stomach. Nothing I could put my finger on exactly.

"She's probably picked up a virus," Joanne volunteered, spearing a forkful of salad. "I mean, who else would be caught out in that cold rain with just her sweater on? Only Betsy—unprepared as usual for the rotten weather any reasonably bright person could see was coming." My sister is a freshman at Westfall Community College. She's majoring in health sciences, and she thinks she knows everything.

"Thanks a *lot*." I made it as sarcastic as I could.

"Joanne has a point," Dad stuck in. "A little more foresight would—"

At that instant the phone rang.

"I'll get it," I said, leaping to my feet.

I do wish you'd tell your friends not to call during mealtime," Mom's voice floated after me. "It's really so disruptive."

"Hello," I practically yelled into the receiver.

"Ouch," Sandy came back. "There goes my eardrum."

"Oh—hi, Sandy."

"Such enthusiasm," she said. Then, "You planning to be busy tonight?"

"No-ooo."

"Mind if I come over?"

I really didn't. I certainly had plenty to talk

about, situations and feelings to straighten out in my mind. And maybe she did, too.

Later we got together in my bedroom. I'd blended us a couple of milkshakes—vanilla for Sandy, strawberry for me.

I flopped down on my bed. Sandy slouched down in my armchair and quickly downed her shake. Apparently, adoration of Josh had not fazed her appetite. I took my time.

She glanced at my melting shake, which was sitting on the floor beside the bed, then eyed me. "Bad as that, huh?"

I shrugged.

"Permit me a wild guess. The team of Marsh and Carney is beginning to cause you extreme pain."

It wasn't as simple as that. I tried to explain—to myself as well as Sandy. "I must admit he's really not that bad. He's friendly, he's got a good sense of humor, and I'd be the first to concede he's a fabulous artist. Of course, he *looks* like an awful joke. That wild hair—the clothes you'd swear he slept in—" I halted in midsentence. Then, "Did you hear that? It's, like, here I go again! Why can't I at least *tolerate* him?

"There's just something about Rob Carney that brings out the monster in me. It's become second nature to *say* things—*do* things—" I dropped the straw into my shake and stirred it around, brooding. "I'm not proud of what I've been saying and doing to him. But—I can't seem to stop it."

"Betsy, Rob isn't exactly blameless, you know. He's been pushing himself on you for so long that he's become a constant irritation. A permanent mosquito bite. And if you strike out at him once in a while, that's the chance he's taking."

"You're absolutely right. I'm like an obsession with him. And yet—"

"And yet what?"

I shrugged my shoulders. "I'm not sure, exactly." Slowly I tried to explain what I was feeling, that for the first time, back there in the magazine library, Rob and I had labored, without pain, on the same side of the fence. We had shared our skills, and we had worked happily together. And then we'd pushed ourselves away from Windy Walpole and company, our eyes had met, and the good moments were over.

Sandy drank the last of her vanilla shake before volunteering an opinion. "If I understand you," she said, "you're telling me that you want to experience the creative pleasure of working with Rob without having to put up with the normal—otherwise known as annoying—side of Rob Carney. Am I connecting?"

"Well—I—"

"In other words, you want to keep working with him, but you don't want him bothering you. Well, I think there's an obvious solution, but it means that you'll have to be very straightforward with Rob, spell out, once and for all, your ground rules. And because he's just as taken with these Walpoles as you are, I'll bet anything he'll be willing to control his temptation to bug you. Which is to say, he'll back off. If that's what you really want."

"But—*how*?"

"Any way you can. Try being reasonable, if you think it will get through his thick skull. If not, work your way up to an ultimatum."

I'd never felt comfortable with ultimatums. My usual style is to sound off, then regret it. Or to complain loudly to the family or

29

anyone else who will listen. Or, when pressed enough, to retreat.

All right, I'd find a way to do it if I had to step on Rob's neck to get the message through. The project had become very important to me. "It's easy for you to give advice," I reminded Sandy. "You're the one who lucked out when it came to partners. Josh Amberston. Wow!"

"I guess." Sandy stared off into space. "He certainly does gum up sensible thinking with those gorgeous eyes of his. But—" Her gaze returned to me. "One thing I have learned. People aren't always what they appear to be. And neither are situations. I'm trying to keep my head clear and the smart part of me on track. But sometimes . . ." She let her sentence trail off, then glanced nervously at her watch. "Uh-oh." She got up from the chair, grabbed her coat, and shrugged into it.

"Hey, wait," I said. "This was supposed to be an exchange of views and wisdoms. So far, I've done most of the gabbing, and you've been stuck with the listening and advising." I sat up straight on the bed and locked my fingers around my knees. "Your turn."

She hesitated. And then, "Maybe one of

these days I'll take you up on that—when I've figured some things out first." She headed for the door. I let her go.

I sensed her confusion. I had been tempted to pry. But Sandy and I had known each other for nearly forever. I knew she'd get around to talking after a while. And I'd be there, waiting, when she did.

Chapter Three

The two-week deadline for the rough draft concept was fast approaching, and during that time were such unfun things as a horrendous test in chemistry and another in math III, a subject that had me thoroughly confused until right before the test, at which point I kind of caught on and actually skimmed through the exam with a C+. I fumbled through those days lured on only by good old sixth period—visual arts.

Snags developed with some of the projects. For instance, Mike Hennessey and Bill Goldbloom had settled on a series of political cartoons. The problem was their politics were about as compatible as fire and water. Things between them got so bad that Mr. Baldwin had to suggest they do a series of single-gag cartoons. And they did very well with them, I might add. And then a really great team, Wendy Abel and Jeanette Brill, who started out with such high hopes, discovered that, without knowing it, they'd been dating the same guy. Tempers got so hot that a new partner was found for each girl. But, artistically, it would never be the same.

That very first week I took Sandy's advice and laid down some rules for Rob. It was while we were sketching a rough draft of the first strip. "By the way, Rob," I started.

He glanced up, his pencil still touching the paper. "Yeah?"

"Do you get the same feeling I do about the strip? I mean, Windy and Hannah and Rosalie are absolutely *perfect* characters. I think we've got something really great here."

"Hey, yeah. Good to hear you say that." His eyes narrowed. I could almost see his brain questioning, *What's she up to?* And then he smiled, a small smile at first, broadening into a wide grin.

Was he picking up the wrong message? I did some rapid reassessing, then decided to give him the benefit of the doubt and continue with Plan A. "And I must admit we do work well together."

The wide grin lingered.

"You want it to stay that way—don't you?"

"Are you kidding?"

"Good," I said. "Then I'm sure you'll be glad to hear that I intend to go along with this team thing until the end. On certain conditions." I caught his gaze and held it. "This means—you'll stay off my back. You'll keep a certain distance. You won't take advantage of the situation." I measured my words. "We both know what I'm talking about—don't we?"

A beat in time, while Rob digested that. Then, "Sure," he said. "Gotcha."

He'd said it so cheerfully. What was *really* going on inside that head? Or had years of "too much Rob Carney" made me suspect everything that came out of his mouth?

Even with those doubts, I couldn't deny what was going right with our comic strip.

Dreaming up ideas—especially humorous ones—can be unbelievably tough when you're facing a deadline. It's as if somebody is pointing a finger at you and commanding, "OK, kid, be funny!" Even when you have a rotten cold, a toothache that's so bad you can't eat, you're supposed to think, seven more days to deadline—six more days . . .

Of course, for the first deadline, Mr. Baldwin wasn't asking the impossible. Only for decent "roughs," which meant Rob's less-than-finished cartoons and my not-quite-sharp dialogue. But the quality of Windy emerged and shone through.

The first week we worked in the magazine library and in visual arts class. But it was obvious that we needed to spend time working outside of school. But where?

"I'd volunteer my dad's den," Rob said, "except you'd get lurid ideas, like thinking I was—taking advantage of the situation." He flashed me a huge grin that remained on his face so long that I answered with one of my own.

I was in the mood to return his grin. He'd been pretty good about living up to his end of our deal. Oh, he'd sneak a simmering glance at me now and then—when he thought I wasn't looking. And sometimes he'd sit closer than I'd normally consider safe. But with our strips coming along so well, I didn't think I should make an issue of such minor matters.

"Of course we have only five days left," he reminded me, rubbing his chin and eyeing the ceiling. "And we still have that Sunday strip."

I racked my brain, trying to come up with some place reasonably civilized to work in the evenings.

"I suppose we could use the Marsh family dining room table to lay our stuff out on," I said. "It would have to be after the dinner dishes are cleared and the family's busy with prime-time TV."

Rob snapped his fingers. "Hey! A good possibility." And then, with grin fading, "Ah, but gee, Betsy, that would be imposing."

"I'll just explain the importance of it to my mother. I'm sure she'll understand," I said.

Which meant I had to do a selling job on Mom.

"What?" she hollered. "That Carney boy, *here*? After all the years of harassment he's put you through?"

"Well—harassment is a little—strong—"

"Give it another name, it's still the same." Her mouth froze into a position that said I'd better argue my case well, or forget it.

I hurriedly stressed the approaching deadline, making a special point of our need for a flat surface large enough to lay out our roughs in some order. In short, the dining room table. And when Mom's mouth loosened a little, I whipped out some of our recent roughs and explained, in glowing terms, where our story line was going.

Windy caught her fancy. She actually started to smile. And Hannah's ridiculousness almost cracked her up. Her finger paused over Rosalie. "Very nice," she said. And then she said, frowning, "Haven't I seen that girl somewhere?" She traced the outline of the delicately molded face. "Maybe the expression in the eyes. Or the way she stands."

"Think 'fawn,' " I said.

"That could be it." But her finger was slow to move. "I suppose it's OK," she said after a minute. "If you're sure he'll behave himself."

"Oh, he will."

Rob showed up on our doorstep with his crammed-full accordion-pleated folder under one arm. He'd combed his hair. And he'd traded his usual beat-up sneakers for a pair of shiny brown leather shoes. His pants actually fit, and his oxford cloth shirt was new. It was a rare sight.

Mom left out a plate of her molasses cookies to keep us going as we worked, then the family went into the living room, allowing Rob and me an opportunity to dump and sort our paperwork. I separated the sheets into six piles.

With five daily strips, each having only three panels, we couldn't exactly develop the world's most complex story line. The twelve-paneled Sunday strip gave us at least a fighting chance. Anyway, I did dream up a weekday strip plot to showcase the main characters. In the first panel Windy was portrayed huddled inside his ramshackle cabin, eyes drooping like a basset hound's, looking pretty glum as he puffed on his giant cigar. The balloon above him read, "Hannah, what're we gonna do about the daughter?" The next panel introduced homely Hannah sticking her head into the living room, her balloon reading, "Fix her up and try to find her a *man*." Then the last panel showed this sweet young thing poised shyly at the edge of the doorway.

That was our opening. We carried that plot idea forward: Windy and Hannah scurried around, looking for a man for their daughter—not realizing until the end that the beautiful but bashful Rosalie had latched onto a winner all by herself.

There must be something fascinating about two people totally absorbed in their work because before long, Rob and I began to collect spectators, starting with my eleven-year-old brother, Teddy, who is a grade ahead of Rob's sister, Kimberly, in Summerfield Middle School. The fact that Kimberly and Teddy fought like a couple of stray cats apparently hadn't warded him off.

Teddy is a questioner from way back. He watched, almost quietly, for a while as Rob worked on a panel, then he tugged at Rob's sleeve. "Hey, how come you like doing that stuff so much?"

Rob's fingers strayed to the faces on the paper and brushed away a few cookie crumbs. "When I draw," he said, "it's like I'm king in the land of Windy Walpole. The guy walks because I've created legs for him to walk with. Hannah talks because I created that big mouth of hers. Those trees, that broken-down house, Rosalie's hair, her eyes—they all exist because I made them." He smiled up at Teddy. "Get it?"

Rob's answer may have satisfied Teddy, but it didn't satisfy me. I turned on him. "What about my words and ideas? Are you saying they don't count for much? They come in second-best to some squiggles on a piece of paper?"

"No, of course not. All I'm saying is—"

"I have noticed," I said, "that most of you cartoonists hold the same superior view: 'One picture is worth a thousand words.' How many times have I heard Joe Ansara blurt out that dumb old saying? You guys think you know how it is: head honchos, the cartoonists. The idea people are a couple of inches from the bottom. Right?"

"It's not like that at all," Rob shot back. "We all realize the story line is what moves the action along. Still, a good artist is worth—"

"His weight in gold? Tell me about it, Carney!"

"My, my," from Joanne, who had moved in and was glancing through the roughs, "aren't we getting testy?"

"More cookies, anyone?" my mother's voice sailed into the dining room. And there

40

she was, refilling the plate, watching as Rob and I reached, together, for a couple of fat ones. My hand got there ahead of his.

"Let the guest go first," Mom said, taking a playful swipe at my hand. "I don't know what's gotten into Betsy tonight," she said to Rob. "She usually has more manners than that."

Rob nodded and smiled—and took a cookie. Teddy wandered away. Mom and Joanne watched Rob drawing for a few more minutes, then they, too, left.

We worked more or less in silence for a while, then Dad wandered by. He showed more interest in what we were doing than I'd expected. It turned out that back in his schooldays he'd tried some cartooning, but nothing had come of it. "These are just great," he said, holding up a couple of roughs and giving them a close look. "I see real talent here." He slapped Rob across the shoulders. "If these roughs are any indication of what you normally turn out, I predict quite a future for you."

So much for Rob and his ability. What about mine?

"Of course, our Betsy has always been

41

good with ideas and words." He dismissed my talent with a wave of the hand. "We know what to expect from her. But *these*—" Another friendly shoulder slap, plus a big smile.

My own father.

By then it was nine-thirty. Time to pack it in, I decided. I put away my part of the project and shoved Rob's sketches over to him; I wasted not one precious moment in aiming him toward the closet where Mom had stashed his jacket.

The rest of the family insisted on crowding around the door as he hollered his farewell and took off down our front walk. "It's been nice meeting you," Dad called out. "Good luck on that Sunday strip." Mom added her cheerful, "When you come back tomorrow night, we'll have cider and doughnuts, if you like them." (Which, of course, he did.) Joanne and Teddy waved good night as if he'd been an old friend. I wiggled a few fingers and said nothing.

"Nice boy," Dad said, closing the front door, shutting out the big farewell scene at last.

"Much nicer than Betsy led us to believe," Mom said.

"Yeah," Teddy chimed in. "Much nicer." He gave me a smug grin.

Let's just say that in spite of the increasing chumminess of my family toward Rob and the alternating sizzles and silences I directed at him, he and I got through the rest of that week alive.

By Monday morning we'd arranged the roughs in order, labeled them, and placed our whole show on Mr. Baldwin's desk, democratically mixed in with the other projects. The moment had come to sit back and wait.

"Before I go over these," Mr. Baldwin reported, "I must tell you that I plan to enter the best of the lot in the National Young Cartoonist contest, which is held annually in Syracuse, New York."

A murmur ran through the class.

"All submissions," he added, "must be in Syracuse by December third. The national winner will be announced on the twentieth of December."

He flipped through a few of the comics. We held our collective breaths.

He glanced up and smiled. "I can say,

without a doubt, our top entry will be a tough one to call."

Someone with a case of nerves giggled. Joe Ansara had a coughing fit, and Josh leaned forward, his eyes alert, a small smile on his lips.

Behind me Sandy had come to life. "Fingers crossed?" she whispered next to my ear. She sounded relaxed, her normal good-natured self. But earlier, I'd seen the look she directed at Josh. There hadn't been anything good-natured about it. Something was up between those two. One of these days Sandy and I would have to have that talk, I thought. Definitely.

"About that contest," Josh put in. "What's the top prize?"

"The winning entry will be sent to a well-known national syndicate for appraisal," Mr. Baldwin said. "And the series will appear in several of their newspapers. And that, I needn't remind you, could be the first step to a professional career in cartooning—and, eventually, a tidy income."

"Ah." Josh slid back in his seat. "Great. Just great."

Newspaper syndicates are the only way to

44

make money in the cartooning business. If a comic strip were to be accepted, it would join nearly five hundred others and get distributed to seventeen hundred daily newspapers in this country—and who knows how many overseas. But it was tough just to get work looked at by a syndicate. Unknown cartoonists rarely stood a chance.

That's why the National Young Cartoonist contest was so important. The winners could bypass a lot of the early stages, getting a free ride right to the desk of a top syndicate editor.

"Just for the fun of it," Mr. Baldwin suggested, "why don't I lay out the roughs." He strode to the rear of the class and proceeded to do that on the long table. "Then you can come up here a few at a time, go over them carefully, and form your own opinions."

I'll admit to feeling a bit overinvolved with "Windy," so I made a special effort to concentrate on everybody else's roughs.

Sandy and Josh had done pretty well with "Bo McClure." Sandy had provided some fairly good dialogue for the spookier scenes at the old mansion. And Josh did have a knack for colorful figures, although his material looked a little more primitive than usual. As I poked

45

through their roughs, he hovered nearby, obviously checking for my reaction.

"Very, very nice," I said heartily. "You guys are doing a good job."

Josh rubbed his palms together and beamed like a proud father.

Sandy had made it to "Windy." Which wasn't easy, considering that quite a crowd had congregated at that end of the table. The buzz of voices was hard to miss. And Sandy's familiar alto sounded above all. "These are *fantastic*. I mean, the best." She caught my eye. "You and Rob really did it. That Hannah." She pointed at her and laughed out loud. "Perfect!"

The buzz grew louder and more friendly as other kids worked their way along the table to get a look at "Windy Walpole." Even Rob wandered over to stand around and try to look modest while listening to side comments. If his reaction was anything like mine, what he heard must have made his spirits soar.

Josh took his time about following the herd to "Windy." And when he'd finally glanced through our strips, examining a couple of them close-up, he didn't have much to say. Just, "Not bad." And, "You guys sure put a lot of work into these."

He stood with his feet apart, arms folded across his chest, looking a little grim. Finally he announced to nobody in particular, "I thought Mr. Baldwin told us to work on *roughs*. These panels don't look like roughs to me." He spotted our visual arts teacher. "Mr. Baldwin," he said plaintively, "are they supposed to turn in such finished work so early on? I mean, is it fair to the rest of us who did exactly what you asked us to do?"

Mr. Baldwin shrugged. "This may be their idea of roughs. Besides," he added, "four weeks from now each team will be required to give me their series in finished form. That should tell the story."

The group was starting to break up; most of the kids headed for their seats. Some, like Michelle Blaine, stopped to give Josh a few words of praise.

"Liked yours, too," Michelle murmured, resting a hand on his wrist and pressing it. " 'Bo' shows definite promise."

"Gee, thanks a lot," Josh said, making no move to go back to his seat. I knew what he really meant: *thanks for nothing.*

47

A couple of others made a mild fuss over "Bo McClure." But it was like clapping with mittens on.

"Josh?" said Sandy, who had moved closer to him and was arranging her face in a smile.

He looked beyond her, not smiling at all. And after hesitating she walked stiffly past him to her seat.

I'll say one thing for Rob. He doesn't miss much. "Josh never was good at coming out second-best," he remarked. He gave me a grin that was pure glee.

This was a side of Rob Carney that I'd never realized existed. "Very interesting," I said. "Since when have you been so competitive?"

"Since never." He straightened up slowly, absorbing a new thought. "Until now." Then, "You know, I'm really good at something for the first time in my life. And I *like* it. *Boy*, do I like it!"

"Well, I'm not at all sure I do." I lowered my voice because Josh was standing not all that many feet away, probably feeling very down. Poor Josh. He'd been so sure that their strip would be the center of attention.

Josh was leaning against the wall by the windows, picking at his thumbnail. A lock of his hair had fallen over one eye, and the corners of his mouth were turned down. Disappointment hung over him like a dark cloud. I could identify with that.

"Well, at least you could have some compassion for Josh," I said.

"Compassion?" he echoed. "For Josh Amberston, star first baseman for Summerfield High's Blue Falcons? Josh, who had the lead in the drama club's musical last year? Josh, of the perfect features and the barbell muscles? Ah, come *on*, Betsy—"

"Shh, he'll hear you!" My fingers itched to smooth back that lock of hair from Josh's forehead. Lucky for me I don't let my fingers do everything they want to. But I did glide over, intending to murmur something upbeat. That is, I would have, if he hadn't stalked in the other direction to plunk into his seat.

"That's Josh for you," Rob muttered. "A real gracious loser."

Still, I felt funny about it. Did Josh have a valid point? It was true that Rob and I had sharpened "Windy Walpole" to a stage beyond primitive roughing. Were we subconsciously trying to outshine Josh, Sandy, and the others? Trying to show them up?

I mentioned this idea to Rob after class.

"Since when is doing your best called 'showing them up'?" he demanded. "Let's get this straight. Josh and Sandy and all the other kids have four more weeks to develop their material and prove who's got the real stuff. That's the same four weeks you and I have. Do you plan on blowing "Windy Walpole" on the basis of some dumb theory?"

"Well, put that way—no."

Chapter Four

Word travels fast in a small-town school like Summerfield High. The possibility of anybody local actually having a fighting chance at winning in a national contest—and a fun thing like a cartoon contest, at that—was the topic of the week. And the talk going around was that "Windy Walpole" had something special going for it.

Rob and I were back to our old spot in the magazine library, taking over most of the table for our project. But life was no longer just the two of us battling it out across from each other. People would drift in, watch over our shoulders, and offer simpleminded comments. And girls who had previously considered Rob Carney part of the wallpaper had suddenly discovered him. Especially one girl.

Rosemary Teal, who thinks she's Summerfield's answer to Brooke Shields, had become a daily visitor. And she was in no way shy about what she had in mind. I mean, I might just as well have been an unoccupied library chair for her to push away while getting to Rob.

The first few times I tried to overlook Rosemary—which was like trying to overlook Mount Vesuvius during an eruption. While she went through her femme fatale routine with Rob, I doodled in the margins of my notebook and wrote out my initials several dozen times, designing all kinds of fancy letters.

Finally, I couldn't be quiet anymore. "Rosemary," I said one day, leveling my famous cool stare at her, "why don't you get out of here so Rob and I can ink in our Sunday strip?" Another time, to Rob, "All right, Carney, as long as you're wasting time playing games with Wonder Woman here, I'll take myself elsewhere." I paused briefly, then added, "When you're ready to get down to business, call me." And sometimes I *really* left, squeezing into the reading room with Josh and Sandy for a social break.

Equally unpleasant things were going on in those cramped quarters. Like Josh not talking to Sandy. Or was it Sandy not talking to Josh? They would both talk to me, but in those odd, stilted tones that belonged to strangers. So I'd wander back to the magazine room and sit there until Rosemary pulled herself together and went home. Then Rob and I would get back to work.

In one area we had made some progress. Rob was keeping his distance, just as he said he would. Oh, he was friendly enough, but he no longer went out of his way to push even closer. That had to be an improvement. Yet, sometimes—sometimes I found myself missing the old Rob. Scratch that. Let's just say, I'd spent so many years fending off that skinny, wild-haired, unpressed specimen I'd always known, there had to be moments of loss. Like the pesky little cousin who bothers you constantly when he comes for the weekend and whom you miss afterward because you'd finally gotten used to him by Sunday afternoon.

The year before, Rob had asked me to our

school's pre-Thanksgiving bash, the November Harvest Ball; I'd given him the big ha-ha—as I had the year before that. I'd ended up going to the dance with Allen Sears, who is two inches shorter than I am and who had a cold that kept him blowing his nose throughout that otherwise totally unmemorable evening.

One afternoon as Rob and I hunched over the library table, inking in the last panel of the Sunday strip, I wondered if he would take his chances and invite me to the ball this year. And if he did, would I actually consider going?

The first question was answered in no uncertain terms with the arrival, yet again, of Rosemary Teal.

She had done some work on herself. Rinsed her hair, changing it from a shade of ash blond to light brown. Gone in for heavier doses of eye makeup. Made her lips full and raspberry red. Wiggled herself into a turquoise sweater a size too small. And she had come with a purpose. She used her most persuasive voice to ask Rob if he would accompany her to the November Harvest Ball.

"For heaven's sake, Rosemary," I snapped, "don't you have any couth at all?"

"Just because I invited Rob to the ball?" Her eyes widened. "My goodness, Betsy, are you still living in the Stone Age? Since when is it wrong for a modern woman to ask her man to a school function?"

Her man.

"Besides," she said, "I wasn't asking you, I was asking Rob." She gave him a big smile. "Well? What's the good word?"

But I wasn't finished. "I don't care what you ask Rob, but this is neither the time nor the place to make your pitch. Why don't you wait until—"

"Betsy," she cut in, "why don't you get off my back?"

There was an electric silence as we glared at each other. Then we both turned our eyes toward Rob, who—just sat there, playing with his pen and humming under his breath. He inked in the half-moon on his fingernail and admired it before gazing in our general direction. "Well, now, I'll tell you," he drawled, "my theory is that he travels fastest who travels alone. So-ooo"—he grinned—"I'm going by myself. If it's all right with you girls."

"I couldn't care less," I said.

"That's fine with me," Rosemary said.

"You're not the only guy on my list. In fact," she said, lifting her chin, "Benjy Marmon said that he'd be only too glad to take me. But I just thought I'd give you first chance."

"Right," Rob said heartily. "Well, maybe some other time."

"I don't think so," she said. She opened her mouth to spout something else and sort of choked. Her face turned red.

She turned and left the room quickly, with her head held high. We could hear her shoes clack along the corridor outside the library door, then speed up as she broke into a run. I got the distinct impression that Rosemary wouldn't bother us again. Which shows how much I had to learn.

I was still sizzling over Rob's "if-it's-all-right-with-you-girls" remark. Why did he think it mattered to me if he went to the dance without a date? Nothing about his comment had set right with me. He had to sense my irritation.

I finished my share of the inking—in as much silence as I could decently muster. Then I put on my coat and, without waiting for Rob, got out of there as quickly as possible.

*   *   *

Sandy didn't phone first, she just came over. And I could see immediately that she had a few things on her mind.

Most of them boiled down to Josh Amberston. "He's impossible," she said. "Which means self-indulgent with a one-track mind and totally unable to admit he can be wrong." And she bit into one of the candied apples we'd raided from the refrigerator— along with a couple of ham sandwiches and ice-cream bars. When Sandy gets angry or upset, she eats. Fortunately, she doesn't get that upset that often.

We were in my bedroom, at our usual posts: Sandy, slumped in the upholstered chair, me, stretched along the bed, with the back of my head resting against the head-board. I was listening, but not quite buying. I mean, sometimes anger colors a person's ability to see clearly, right? There had to be more to Josh than the few little faults she'd listed.

"Oh, sure, there's more all right." She took a few bites of the ham sandwich, then put it down on my night table and started in on her ice-cream bar. "I could go on about Josh Amberston all night."

I waited for her to finish the ice cream

before she continued talking. At times you have to do that with Sandy.

"You should hear him sound off about 'Windy Walpole,' " she said. "Let's face it, Josh is definitely not a good loser. And when the other kids all went over to the other end of that table, leaving our 'Bo' hanging there, he was very upset."

"Disappointed, at least," I acknowledged. "But listen, you two still have time to get ahead. The finished product is what counts. You heard Mr. Baldwin."

"Josh blames my story line. He says the plot is the usual old stuff and my dialogue's not exciting enough. I blame his sketches. I told him they're too crude. And I told him he's not sensitive enough to catch onto my story line and fit his cartooning to my dialogue. Of course, that was after he put the writing down—"

"Hey," I cut in, "it's just a contest. Maybe we should all repeat that to ourselves ten times a day. We're all students, learning, having fun while we do the best we can."

There was silence, while we polished off both sandwiches. Then I ventured cautiously,

"I had sort of figured you and Josh would be going to the Harvest Ball together."

She sat up straight. "Are you kidding? No *way* would I go to that dance with him!"

So, she didn't have to yell.

"Actually," she went on with less heat, "Benjy Marmon asked me this morning, and I accepted."

Benjy? Rosemary's man?

She looked at me from under her lashes. "And you'll be going with—Allen Sears?"

"We both know better."

"Give me one more guess." She tapped a finger against her forehead. "It's coming—coming—I've *got* it." Ear-to-ear smile. "You finally said yes to Rob."

A pause, while I gathered myself together. "As a matter of fact, no."

"What? You mean after all these weeks, you still haven't overcome that childish prejudice? The guy's terrific, Betsy. Haven't you noticed how many girls in school look twice now when Rob Carney goes by?"

Of course I had. I wasn't blind.

"Well, then, why—" She stopped. "Oh, I get it," she said. "The real issue is that he

59

didn't ask you to go with him. Am I right? Rob *didn't* ask you?"

"Well—"

"Ah, so. Am I now supposed to guess who the lucky girl is?"

"Try nobody."

"He's not going to the ball? Or he's going alone?"

"You've got it. He's going by himself."

"Wow, this could be a most interesting situation. If you show up alone, he shows up alone, who knows what might happen? Some great romances have started that way. Eyes meet across the crowded dance floor—"

"Hey, forget it. The day I trade passionate glances with Rob Carney will be the most unlikely day of my life. If nobody asks me, well, I just won't go. It's as simple as that."

The conversation came to a lull shortly afterward. When Sandy left for home, I could tell she was feeling pretty happy. And why not? She had rid herself of a lot of pent-up frustration, and she'd let me know, in a not-so-subtle way, about Benjy and her. And she'd tried to set me up with Rob. What are friends for? It had turned into one of her better evenings.

Good for Sandy. Not so good for me.

I considered going downstairs and talking to my sister. After that I considered studying some math, then brushing my teeth and going to bed.

What I did instead was ease to within hearing distance of the upstairs phone, prop a paperback romance on my knees, and keep my eyes on the pages and my ears alerted for the phone. Because—sometimes—certain people called after nine.

I'd wait until ten. Then I'd forget the whole really stupid idea and head for bed.

The phone rang, piercingly clear, at nine forty-five. "I'll get it," I hollered down. And in a flash I'd grabbed the receiver. "Hello!"

It was a guy. But it didn't sound at all like—a certain person. I lowered my tone to a dignified, "Yes?" Just in case. I mean, it could be *anybody*.

"It's me. Josh."

A feeling that I couldn't quite interpret washed through me. Not disappointment. I mean—*Josh*? How could that be a disappointment? It was just that I'd been assuming—

"Oh, hi, Josh. What's up?"

"About the November Harvest Ball." He cleared his throat. "You going with anybody?"

"Well, actually, no."

"Good. I was afraid Carney would—*you* know—take advantage of the fact you're working together and pressure you." Pause. And then, "Unless he already asked you, and you turned him down?"

What could I say? A mumble seemed to fit nicely.

"OK, then I'm asking. Will you go with me?"

Self-indulgent, Sandy had called him. One-track. Never admits to being wrong . . .

I'd had my eye on this really stunning gold lamé dress on display at a downtown department store, figuring—just in case—

"Well?"

Where was that little flip of the heart I'd always experienced when I'd dreamed of Josh and me going anywhere, doing anything, together?

"Hey, you still there?"

On the other hand, last year there had been Allen Sears. . . . "I'm sorry. Yes, I'm still here. And, yes, I'd like to go with you."

Chapter Five

I saved the news for the breakfast table next morning.

"Josh Amberston?" Joanne gave me one of those you've-got-to-be-kidding smiles. Still, I could see she was impressed. It isn't every day that my sister is impressed with something I do.

"Amberston," my mother echoed, handing me a plate with scrambled eggs and toast on it. "Does he live on Woodward Road? Sam and Julie Amberston's son? Tall, good-looking boy with a deep voice?"

"One and the same," I said, taking a bite of toast.

"Well—" Mom said, searching for words. "He certainly is easy on the eyes."

Easy on the eyes. Was that the best she could come up with?

"Boy, you did OK for a change." Teddy approved. "That guy's really something. Did you see the ball game against the Roseland High Warblers? Amberston hit a two-bagger that brought in the winning run. Wow!"

I grinned. So far, so good.

"Although," Teddy added, "I'm kind of surprised. I thought sure you'd be going with Rob. That would be even more OK. How come you're not?" And when I didn't answer, he continued, "Of course Rob isn't a big hero, or a Mister Muscle, and he doesn't look all that special. But . . ." His voice trailed away.

Joanne set down her fork. I could see the same questions surfacing inside her head. If those questions got too pointed, I would be forced to admit more than I'd planned. And because my plans didn't include a discussion of Rob Carney, I concentrated on my breakfast, eating as quickly as I could.

That morning as I was on my way to school, Josh caught up with me at the corner where Woodward Road meets Locust Avenue. I was surprised because I didn't usually run into him in the morning. He slung his arm over my shoulder—making us an instant twosome to anyone who happened by. We ambled along the sidewalk of Locust like Siamese twins joined at the hip. It was all very cozy.

"Hey, look, there's Carney!" Josh's grin was wide, almost welcoming. He let go of me long enough to wave. It was unusual for Josh to be that cordial to Rob.

Not that it appeared to disturb Rob. He was doing a sort of balancing act along the curb, taking time off only to wiggle some fingers in our direction. Tucked under one arm were his books and the beat-up pleated folder. The folder looked pretty bulky. And why not? Our stack of "Windy Walpole" papers had been growing daily, changing from the semirough state of a few weeks before to a really classy look.

"Oh, by the way," Josh said, "did I tell you I passed my driver's test? I'll be able to pick you up the night of the dance."

He hadn't even told me he'd had a learner's permit, which says a lot about how often Josh and I discussed the details of our lives.

We parted at the school entrance. "See

you later," he promised. There was a pro-longed moment of eye-to-eye contact, during which Josh's dark, heavy-lashed eyes looked straight into mine. I faltered, then glanced away.

I'd read about those moments in romances. How when a guy looks deep into a girl's eyes this sudden chill of anticipation runs up her spine, and her heart beats furiously, and waves of ecstasy and longing race through. I guess what it boils down to is that you shouldn't believe everything you read.

Sandy and I got together in the cafeteria after fourth period. That's when I had planned on telling her about Josh asking me to the Harvest Ball. I felt a little guilty about going with Josh. Even though Sandy had said she wouldn't want to go with him, I wasn't con-vinced she really meant it.

I wasn't the one to tell her first, however. I could tell by the way she looked at me that the school grapevine had worked again.

We were seated at a corner table, unload-ing our trays, before the subject came up. "Josh Amberston of all people," Sandy said.

"Well, you said there was no way you'd go

out with him if he asked you," I said. I hadn't meant to be so defensive.

"I wouldn't. But I didn't expect you to go out with him, either. Betsy, sometimes I wonder about you."

"Well, don't," I said. "All brain cells are operating just fine."

She attacked her casserole with vigor. "Don't you even question his motives?"

"It takes a devious motive for a guy to ask me to a dance?" That bothered me. "Friend to friend, what are you trying to tell me?"

She backed down a little after that, muttering something about not trusting Josh or not wanting to see me get hurt, I forget which—and we went back to eating, each thinking her own thoughts.

The truth was, Josh had never before shown any special interest in Betsy Marsh, girl in the fifth seat of the middle row in visual arts. Aside from our mutual interest in cartooning, we were more or less talking acquaintances—"Hi, How are you doing," that sort of thing—except that I'd been doing some private daydreaming about him since early October.

I crunched on a sliver of celery.

"Uh-oh, there goes Vicki Sellers. Rob's sliding over—she's moving in next to him—"

"Good grief, can't he do better than *that*? She's such a—such a—" I searched my brain trying to come up with the right word. No decent one came.

"Oh, I guess Vicki does get around. But all the guys say she's a lot of fun on a date. And who knows"—Sandy downed the last of her milk—"maybe that's what Rob needs right now. A little fun in his life. Listen, is it possible he'll not go solo and ask Vicki to the dance instead?"

What could I say? There'd been a day, not so long ago, when I'd pretty much known how Rob would react to any situation involving girls. Times had changed. I no longer had a clue.

This whole cartoon business was doing wonders for Rob's ego, and he seemed to be turning into a completely new person.

Vicki and Rob did exit the cafeteria together. That is, he got up to leave, and she looped an elbow around his waist, hugging him to her, following his every step, and laughing all the way out the cafeteria door.

Was he actually enjoying that display? Or

was that a look of pure embarrassment I'd seen color his face?

"Now there goes a guy who's learning to enjoy himself," Sandy said. "I say, more power to him."

"And I say—" Nothing. Because I'd made a choice. Business, as usual; personal involvement, out. That meant Rob could hang out with anyone he liked, and I would say nothing about his choice of company. I'd stick to that—if I could.

Sixth period brought our teams together for yet another session. We were, in most ways, the same old class we'd been when we started visual arts, talking when we should be listening, forgetting class assignments, playing outrageous jokes on one another, arguing, kidding, sulking, and making noise. In other less obvious ways, however, we'd changed. There was a sense of urgency in the class now. Serious business was at hand.

That day Mr. Baldwin checked out the progress of all our cartoons, and we all had a quick chance to look at one another's work. After he had finished, Mr. Baldwin sat down in his swivel chair, leaned back, and pressed his fingertips together. "Possible choices for the contest are now open for discussion. Any opinions, based on what you've seen so far?"

Everybody had an opinion. And what they all added up to was a lot of noise. But nowhere in the lively discussion did the adventure strip "Bo McClure" come up. Sandy appeared perfectly at home with this. But given Josh's feelings about their creation, I knew he had to be hurting.

"All right," Mr. Baldwin said, "does any particular series stand out so far?"

"'Windy,'" Jeanette Brill called out. There was a chorus of "yeahs."

Over by the windows Rob's face had lit up. I made a special effort to catch his eye, returning his grin with a bright smile of my own. We'd put a lot of time and energy into making "Windy Walpole" a little different, a little better than the others. An answering smile seemed the least I could do for my partner.

"Aha," Sandy chirped behind me. "Do I detect an emotional moment between partners?"

I turned around and glared at her.

"A month from now," she continued cheerfully, "remember I said it first."

At the end of the visual arts period, Josh

slid up close to me while we were filing past the door. "OK if I come over tonight?"

"Sure," I said. "I'll be home all evening." Then I added, "Mom usually makes popcorn, and we can split a couple of my famous milk shakes, watch TV, and just relax and have some fun." It was a good idea for Josh to come over. Dad could get a chance to meet him, and the others could get to know the *real* Josh.

"Sounds great," Josh said. "See you around seven."

Josh, at my house. Greeting the family. Sharing popcorn and making small talk as he sat next to me on the sofa. And—if the family scattered, as they usually did on Friday nights—maybe just the two of us on that sofa. Alone.

The built-in possibilities sent a tremor along my ribs to a spot just under my chin. The area seemed vaguely familiar. Was this what the romances were referring to when they spoke of the "pulse beat trip-hammering at the base of the throat"?

When I got to the magazine library that afternoon, the pulse beat, or whatever, was long gone, and I found myself looking forward to sharing time with my partner in creativity.

Rob had arrived ahead of me, and he appeared grim. Or "icy, with whiffs of distress." Better yet, just plain old "sour." He set down his inking pen. "Well, it's about time you got here," he said. "Everybody else on the second floor is slaving away at their material except us."

Not like Rob at all. Hmmm.

"If we're going to win this contest, you've got to get with it," he added.

"Well!" I said. "Since when am I supposed to report to you?"

"You don't see Sandy and Josh showing up fifteen minutes late," he fumed. "In fact, Josh showed up five minutes early. Right after I got here. And he was bursting with all sorts of fun facts—about your date with him tonight, and how you're going to spend the whole evening together, popping corn, and—"

"Aah," I said. A glimmer. "*That's* it. You don't approve of what I do in my free time, away from the cartoon. Well, if we're going to get into that sort of sport, it should be equal time for equal partners. Although I wouldn't *dream* of making an issue of your little scene in the cafeteria at lunchtime."

"Scene? What scene?"

"You know perfectly well what scene. Vicki Sellers hanging onto you like a leech, and giggling. I mean, *really*, Rob." So much for not saying anything about Rob's choice of company.

"Aw, come on. Vicki does that with all the guys. That's her style. Of course, if I'd known it was going to *bother* you—"

"Bother me? Don't be ridiculous! I just think, in the interest of common sense, you'd—"

"Oh, it's common sense we're talking about? And you figure hanging out with Josh is sensible."

I think at that instant we really heard ourselves. We both stopped as if struck. I said it first. "What are we doing?"

Rob ran his fingers through his hair. "Something awfully dumb," he said.

We sat there quietly. Rob doodled on his sketch pad, and I stared blindly at the cover of the latest issue of *Newsweek*.

After a while he said, "Maybe we should get down to business."

73

"Right," I said.

We were still at it when Sandy and Josh came out of the reading room. I glanced up, smiled, and said, "Hi." Rob didn't glance up. And he said nothing at all.

We worked until Mrs. Benton made a point of jangling her keys under our noses. And then Rob and I went our separate ways.

What can I say about the Friday evening that Josh came over to meet the family? Considering how it went, almost anything I say will be too much. Meaning, I've spent more exciting evenings examining my fingernails.

For reasons that escape me, the family stuck around—even Teddy, who normally disappears just before it's time to clear the dinner table. And the conversation ranged from Teddy's endless prattle about last spring's Blue Falcons and double plays and earned run averages to Dad's sharp questions, meant to ferret out the darker corners of Josh's personality. Mom and Joanne just plain hung around.

We watched a James Bond rerun on TV because Josh was hung up on James Bond thrillers. And we actually did occupy the sofa together—with chatty Teddy squeezed in between us.

Altogether a bust of an evening. I could only hope the November Harvest Ball would be an improvement.

Chapter Six

On Monday afternoon an old college room-mate of Mr. Baldwin's showed up at our visual arts class. His name was Harlow Whitney, and his cartoon strip, "Little Eli," had found a home in five hundred daily newspapers throughout the country.

"You're in for a treat," Mr. Baldwin told us, rubbing his palms together and beaming. Then, "Harlow, the stage is yours."

If you've never seen a cartoon character come to life at the hands of a professional, you've really missed something.

Mr. Baldwin had set up some white poster board on an easel. Harlow Whitney approached it, glanced up and down, whipped out a charcoal pencil, and made some quick, sharp strokes. And there he was—"Little Eli," with his big round eyes, and his gap-toothed grin, and the train engineer's cap, and the spotted mongrel pup that always hung around his ankles. Behind Eli were tufts of grass and the beginnings of a house and some outlined trees. A few more strokes and there it all was—a fully populated cartoon strip.

Then he drew us some examples of "visual shorthand," or ways to indicate such things as the wafting aromas of cooking food, the sun edging over the morning's horizon. He showed us how to indicate characters' feelings and emotions: agitation, surprise, anger, and sadness. And we watched him change the shape of the talk balloons to illustrate emotions. He put icicles on the rim of one to show a cold-shouldered snub. And zigzags on another, to show yelling. I'd never have believed how much you could show by changing the balloon.

And then Harlow Whitney started asking us about our projects. Suddenly it turned into show-and-tell time, with all of us sitting back and waiting while he fingered our work.

"Very nice," he said. A little later, "Good

clean job." Later yet, glancing up, "A lot of original thinking here." And then he got to "Windy Walpole."

I met Rob's gaze. He smiled, but I could see he was feeling unsettled. I mean, the man was a *professional*. We had to respect any opinion he might give, good or bad.

"I understand this class will be submitting an entry to the contest in Syracuse," he said.

Mr. Baldwin nodded yes.

He held our folder high. "This one," he said, "will make out just fine."

Harlow Whitney had spoken his piece.

I could see Rob collapse against his chair and close his eyes. My own felt watery around the edges. I rubbed at them, but it did nothing for the sudden blur.

"Hey, haven't I said that all along?" Joe Ansara hollered out. Somebody in the last row clapped. And the other kids took it from there. At least, *most* of them did.

Smiling to himself, Mr. Baldwin gathered the projects and stacked them on the shelves behind his desk.

Soon the visual arts period was over, Harlow Whitney had gone on his way, and the rest of us had moved on to our next classes. And an hour later the school day had worked itself to a close.

But not for Rob and me. We'd returned to our usual places in the magazine library and were busily reworking several panels to include Harlow Whitney's "visual shorthand." As Rob said, if you're determined to be good, why not try for better?

Josh stopped at our table shortly before lock-up time. "You two still at it? Sandy and I finished for good a couple of minutes ago. And, boy, is that relief. Even if he never wins some old contest, I'm pretty pleased with Bo."

"Good for you," Rob muttered, inking in Rosalie's hair. "We're still upgrading our strips."

Josh eyed Rosalie's progress, then leaned forward. "Hey," he said, "that girl looks sort of familiar. Anyone we know?"

"Just a figment of my overripe imagination," Rob answered cheerfully. "You might call her the girl of my dreams."

"If you say so," Josh said. Then, to me, "I've got my dad's car for the afternoon. Need a lift home?"

"Not me," Rob said, wiping his pen clean, then standing up and yawning.

"Well, actually, I wasn't asking you. Betsy, what do you say?"

There was a hushed interval while I watched Rob open his mouth as if about to say something. Then he closed his mouth, gathered his stuff together, reached for his jacket, and drawled, "Have a fun trip, you two. Don't do anything I wouldn't do." And he left. Just like that.

Not that I really cared.

For the record, the trip in Josh's car was just fine. We took the long way home, stopping at BurgerMaster for a couple of hamburgers, then cruising along some back roads, where Josh turned on some music and stopped the car near a grove of trees. We talked about school stuff and the coming November Harvest Ball. We didn't discuss Sandy—although I was dying to—because he quashed that subject as soon as I brought it up. And we didn't talk about cartoon strips because I could see where that would get us, and it was nowhere good.

After we'd run out of things to talk about, Josh put his arm around me and kissed me. It was an expert job. I mean, I'd been kissed before, and I could tell experienced from inexperienced. And believe me when I say Josh knew exactly how to go about it. His lips were warm on mine, and urgent. In the middle of all this urgency, a little voice inside me whispered, "Hey! Put the brake on." And I whispered, "No—" and gave Josh a gentle shove, and he quit.

Which didn't bother me half so much as it did Josh, who muttered about it all the way home. I guess he wasn't used to girls who put the brake on.

In the meantime my mother had been making certain decisions of her own. "After the dinner dishes are done," she said as soon as I got past the front door, "you and I are going dress shopping. I saw this really attractive formal in the Westfall Shopping Center. It's plum-colored, with a scoop neckline, cap sleeves, and a large flounce that stretches from the hemline to just over the hips. It comes with a capelet, too. The style would be just perfect for you."

"But, wait," I said, "I've already spotted the perfect dress downtown in a display window. Gold lamé, with really great lines, and—"

"If you're talking about the one I think you're talking about," she said, "I've already seen it. And my feeling is that it's much too old for you. And the color is all wrong. For once in your life, Betsy, listen to me when I say—"

And so it went, more or less continuously through dinner and the dishes. Then off we sprinted to the Westfall Shopping Center.

Sandy was there, too—with *her* mother. When we spotted her, she was busy trying on huge, dangling gold earrings and several layers of arm bangles to go with the emerald-green formal she'd talked her mother into approving.

She jiggled her head, and the earrings flew here and there. "Betsy, what do you think? I mean, be honest."

"Well, Sandy," I said, groping, "I'd say—" It wasn't often that Mrs. James's taste and mine coincided. But this time we both agreed that she looked like a pirate queen.

"I suppose you're getting something in fuchsia," Sandy said. "That's Josh's favorite color."

"Well, not exactly. I've been considering—"

"Or at least something bright. Josh goes for bright, clear colors. Calls them dramatically pure." She dropped the earrings back on the store counter and shook the bangles from her wrist. "I should know. After all, I've spent too many weeks absorbing Josh Amberston's opinions. And he has an opinion on just about every subject going."

Fuchsia. I shrank inside myself.

"I think Betsy should concentrate on a color that brings out her best features," my mother said. "After all, a formal gown is quite an investment. And she'll want to wear it more than once. There will be other dances, other boys asking her. And Josh's opinion is not necessarily a message sent down from on high."

"Oh, I'm sure you have a point, Mrs. Marsh," Sandy said quickly. "I just thought Betsy might want to—"

"Sandra," Mrs. James cut in, "why don't we let Betsy and her mother make the decision? After all, they didn't tell you to pick that gaudy green. Although," she said as she turned to my mother, "it has to be an improvement over the fuchsia with the sequins she insisted on at first."

"Fuchsia?" I looked directly at Sandy. "Well, well," I said.

"It just so happens," she said, not meeting my gaze, "that I also go for fuchsia." She angled her chin upward. "If that's all right with everybody here."

"I guess there's no accounting for color sense."

Mom and I found our way to the formal wear section, where we agonized over several desirables. That is, I agonized, while she stood on one foot then the other, saying, "Come on, Betsy, make up your mind."

I'd eliminated her choice in short order. Blamed it on the flounce. Meaning, I wasn't into flounces that ran from hemline to hipline. I tried on a long, butter yellow gown, then a form-fitting number in muted raspberry. I didn't like either of them. Finally I tried on a cobalt-blue, off-the-shoulder gown with really nice lines.

"That blue does lovely things for your eyes," Mom commented. "Or will my approval kill its chances?" She scrutinized the dress and me.

I looked at myself in the dressing room mirror. Hmmm. It did nice things for me, and

I liked the way the skirt swished when I moved. As for the neckline—well, I'd never been much for off-the-shoulder, but— "I'll take it," I said.

The next day Sandy and I were sitting in my room, talking. She spotted my gown in the closet and went over to look at it. "Blue? I thought you'd go for something more—"

"Fuchsia?"

"But I can see," she said, "that the blue is definitely you."

I could tell there was something else she wanted to say, but the words wouldn't come. And since I wasn't sure I wanted to hear what she had to say, I could wait.

In the meantime the November Harvest Ball was sneaking up fast. To add to the tension I felt about the dance, Rob and I had decided to complete "Windy Walpole" on the Friday before the ball. Harlow Whitney's praise had spurred us on. We both felt the need to make every inked line and word exactly right. And with our Friday deadline just a couple of days away, it wasn't a big surprise that our nerves were slightly frayed.

That Wednesday the magazine library was temporarily off limits because of a water leak, which meant that Rob and I were more or less forced to take over the now-empty reading room that Josh and Sandy had vacated.

I wanted to be big about it and not complain. And Rob said, "If you can take the cramped quarters, I can, too." Cooperation. Anything for the good of the strip. Right?

And then. . . . It started when I dropped a pen and got down on my knees to search under the table for it—only to discover that Rob, too, was down there, hunting among the rug tufts. Our heads clunked. We both backed off. And there we sat, on our haunches, staring at each other like a couple of wary cats on a back fence.

"Hi, stranger," Rob said.

"Uh, hi." My fingers had found the pen. But the rest of me stayed where it was.

Rob made no effort to pull back. In fact, it seemed that he'd come nearer. "Hey," he half whispered, "you know what? This could be, like, a fresh beginning for us." He grabbed for the pen, or my hand, I couldn't tell which. But it didn't matter. Because his face had found my face and was moving in.

And still, I sat—

I heard the slamming of the door first and then Mr. Baldwin's voice. "Something going on here that I should know about?"

Rob, who can move quickly when he has to, yanked the pen from me and backed up until he was clear of the table. Then he stood. "We were, uh, looking for this pen," he said.

Which was true. I mean, that was the original reason. Except, somehow the action had almost gotten out of hand.

"My, isn't it wonderful how some things never change," Mr. Baldwin said, smiling to himself. "I remember a similar moment back in my senior year—"

"Believe me, this isn't one of your similar moments," I said. By then I'd scrambled to my feet, and my mood was darkening. "Rob and I are partners. We've put together what we like to think is a good comic strip, and we're trying to finish it up. That's all there is to it. And take my word for it, Mr. Baldwin, that's all there ever will be."

Rob had retreated to his chair and was scribbling on a piece of paper, very busy all of a sudden. And after waving Mr. Baldwin out of the reading room, I got back to my own work.

We stayed focused on "Windy Walpole" until it was almost closing time, barely acknowledging each other's presence. Then, abruptly, Rob asked, "Did you mean it, about 'that's all there ever will be'?"

I glanced up from my work. His eyes were fixed on me, definitely asking that question and others that were as yet unspoken.

Questions that I had no absolute answers to. Oh, sure, I could say, "Yes, I meant every word." And, "Fresh beginning? Forget it." It would cool him off. And turn him off. Probably forever. And forever was a long time. These days, a person needs every friend she can get.

He stirred in his chair. "Well?"

Outside the reading room door, Mrs. Benton's keys jangled a warning.

Rob shook the panel sheets together and pressed them into his accordion-pleated folder. He capped the ink bottles, put them into a plastic bag, gathered up the pens, then eased himself into his jacket. Then, "We'll talk about this again," he said. "When we have more privacy."

We went through the main exit together, then separated at the corner of Locust by the stop sign. I watched him turn left and hustle up the sidewalk. Then I continued home.

Josh was at my house when I got there. He'd apparently wangled a dinner invitation from Mom; and I could tell by the way he was on the couch, his feet up on my dad's hassock, he figured he was set for the evening. Somehow he'd managed to get Teddy's favorite rerun, "Gilligan's Island," off the TV, and substituted his own shoot-'em-up show. Which hadn't set too well with Teddy, who was slumped in a nearby chair, scowling.

"He's obviously used to getting his own way," Joanne commented to me in the kitchen. "That would really bug me after a while. Of course," she added, "some girls like that in their men. They even look up to a guy who's opinionated and pushy, they consider him macho. Oh, well, Josh, no doubt, has many good qualities. Like, for instance, his fantastic profile."

The image of Rob's so-so profile flashed before me. His nose, stacked up against Josh's, was definitely no contest. And even though he'd taken the trouble to neaten up and tame his hair over the past month, there was just no way that Rob Carney would turn into gorgeous.

Joanne took out some silverware from the drawer. "Of course, fantastic profiles don't really tell the story. You have to take into account a boy's personality."

Personality. I closed my eyes, blotting out Josh's profile and concentrating on his personality.

With Josh you always knew what he liked and what he didn't, and if you didn't happen to agree, that was your problem. Not his. He had little patience for any disagreements.

"And then," Joanne said, "you have to take into account your own personal feelings about the guy."

My personal feelings about Josh and Rob? But before I had time to consider my feelings, Dad's voice came through from the living room, sounding off about the program on the TV. It was time for his favorite early evening news show. Dad said some less than polite things about Josh's show, then changed the channel. Also, I figured he was ticked off about Josh's taking over the hassock.

By the time Joanne and I made it into the

living room, the fireworks had died down; Josh was seated on the recliner, Dad was plunked down in his easy chair with his feet on his hassock, and Teddy had made it back to the sofa.

Josh looked more than a little sour. "About that invite to dinner," he said after a few minutes of glaring straight ahead, "I think I'll pass it up. If you don't mind."

"But, Josh," I said—suddenly struck by the realization that the boy who was supposed to take me to the Harvest Ball was about to leave our house in a huff—"we've already set a place for you at the table! Besides, we should go over certain details for Saturday night, and—"

"If you can't stay, you can't," Dad cut in cheerfully. "Maybe some other time."

Amid the uneasy hush that followed, I walked with Josh to the door. "I—I don't know what to say about Dad," I volunteered. "Except that sometimes he comes home from work very tired, and the least little thing will get to him. But—that's my dad," I finished lamely.

"I've run into fathers like him before," Josh said. "Overprotective, I call them. I can see it bothers him that you go for a guy like me. That's the father in him, I guess." He patted my hand. "But don't you worry about it, Betsy. I'll phone later, and we'll talk about Saturday."

Which I thought was rather generous of him, considering everything.

I returned to the living room and glared at my father. "I hope you're satisfied," I said. "You just drove Josh out."

"Betsy!" my mother said. "Don't speak to your father in that tone of voice!" Then, to Dad, "But I must say, Roy, that really wasn't very nice, you know."

Dad had opened his newspaper to the sports section. He peered over the top of it. "You know, Grace," he said, "you may be right." And then he smiled.

Joanne stalked up to Dad's chair. "About that invite to dinner." A letter-perfect imitation of Josh. "I think I'll pass it up. If you don't mind."

Everybody laughed except me.

At the dinner table I passed the bread, vegetables, and the rest in stony silence. And when Teddy started in about Josh hogging the TV, I silenced him with a glare.

I could see Mom and Dad exchange one of

their significant looks. Then Dad said, "We'll invite the boy over for supper tomorrow. In fact, Betsy, your mother and I will prepare something special." He turned on his let's-make-up expression. "All right with you, chickie?"

Chickie. I hated that outdated nickname. It had been a few years since I was four years old.

Later Joanne caught up with me as I headed for the stairs. "Hold it, sourpuss," she said. "Why are you taking it all so personally? We were only kidding. It's not that Josh is a loser or anything. But even you will admit he can be—"

"There's not that much wrong with Josh," I interrupted. "So he has a few flaws. Don't you? Don't I? And when everyone around here jumps on him like that, it really bothers me. I mean, it's just not fair. And it so happens that I like him." But did I? I knew I sounded defensive.

From back in the living room, Teddy shouted loudly enough for me to hear, "Well, I don't care. Give me old Rob anytime!"

"Just one man's opinion," Joanne said. "I don't necessarily agree with his choice. But then," she added, grinning impishly, "I don't necessarily disagree."

Well, who'd asked them? Certainly not me.

When Josh phoned, I took his call upstairs, making sure that none of the family was listening in. We talked for almost an hour, working out our plans for the Harvest Ball, making pleasant small talk—touching on nothing vital, nothing that would make either of us angry. *Safe* communication. Exactly what a confused mind needs.

I went to bed earlier than usual, staring quietly into the darkness, trying unsuccessfully to sort out the jumble of feelings and emotions that were making my days so unpeaceful.

Standing in my doorway, Joanne called softly. "Betsy? Are you awake?"

I shut my eyes and made my breathing regular. And after a while Joanne went away.

Chapter Seven

We were stuck with the reading room again.

"You'd think, by now, they'd have a simple leak fixed," I said to Rob.

"Who says a leak is simple?"

"All right, *all right.*" I slapped the table with the heel of my hand.

"Ah, yes, it's mighty rough," Rob said, deadpan. He hauled his chair closer to the table, touched my knees with his, then slid away. "Oops, sorry about that," he said. "One of the hazards of the reading room."

Did I detect sarcasm? Rob was getting better at zinging in remarks that I couldn't quite decipher. And he hadn't even bothered to mention the "little talk we'll have later, when we have more privacy." Well, I certainly wasn't going to remind him.

"Hang in there, Betsy," he said. " 'Windy Walpole' should be a finished product after today. The way it's been moving, it looks like we'll make our Friday deadline."

Yes, it would all be over. After almost six complicated weeks, any active contact between Rob Carney and me would be a thing of the past. It would be a relief.

"It's been fun, right?" He looked at me through half-lowered lids. "I haven't put too great a strain on you, have I?"

I said, "Yes, it's been fun, sort of. And, no, the strain hasn't been unbearable." And in most ways that was true.

We worked in companionable silence for a while, applying the final touches to the Sunday strip. At last I put down my pen and glanced up. Rob let go of the panel sheet and caught my eye. And together we said, "Finished!"

We laughed hesitantly, an oddly muted sound that died away almost immediately.

"So," I said. "What will you be doing with your free time now?" It seemed only right to ask. "Hanging out with the other guys at BurgerMaster?"

"Oh, maybe for a little while tonight. After that I'll be busy right through Saturday night. Anne Thomas has asked me to supervise the decorating of the gym for the Harvest Ball. Seems they're planning to go artistic this year, and they figured that—"

"They're perfectly right, of course," I said heartily. I'd give him that much, anyway. But Anne Thomas—last spring's junior prom queen—

"Yeah," Rob read my mind and grinned. "Me and Annie T. There are those who would say I was going up in the world. Well, I say— maybe yes, maybe no."

"She—she's going to the ball with you?"

"No such luck, good or bad. Fact is, I didn't ask her. Although I did hear that she was kind of interested."

"Oh, sure."

He shrugged. "Who knows? Anyway, I'm sticking to the original game plan. Solo. Best way to go." He stood up, stretched, yawned. "Hey, partner, what say we get this show on the road? Tomorrow, at nine sharp, we slip the whole gorgeous business into Baldwin's bottom desk drawer."

We gathered up everything, carefully placed our precious strips in Rob's folder, and headed for the door.

"See you," he said cheerfully.

"You will," I returned equally cheerfully. And we took off down the corridor, splitting at the second-floor water fountain to go our separate ways.

I closed my eyes for a moment, experiencing this sudden need to rest them. When I opened my eyes, Rob was gone.

Josh arrived for dinner that evening—in response to the big invitation—and everyone was terribly proper and polite during the meal. Afterward he declined the opportunity to dial a TV show of his own choosing; he opted instead to take me downtown in his father's car. We ended up at BurgerMaster, more for the social life than the food, since Mom and Dad really had outdone themselves and Josh and I were both stuffed.

November in Summerfield has a bite in the night air that points the way to the inevitable chill, ice, and snow that are coming. I took along my mittens and let Josh turn up the heater. As we got out of the car, snow-flakes danced briskly off the car roof and sprinkled white dust on my hair.

A few of the kids from school had arrived ahead of us. Joe Ansara was playing the video games, while Michelle Blain stood by yelling encouragement. Over in a corner booth Sandy was slurping a giant-sized root beer; across from her sat Benjy Marmon. As we moved in their direction, Benjy made a grab for Sandy's free hand.

Josh muttered, "You'd think they'd be more—more—"

"Discreet?"

"Yeah, that's it. I figured, no matter how impossible Sandy might be in some ways, she at least had enough class not to—not to—" He waved his arms, then let them flop to his sides. "Just shows," he said, "you never do know."

"May I point out that Benjy's hand is covering hers, not vice versa. Although, why it should bother you is beyond me."

"Bother me?" He laughed. " 'Bother' isn't the right word. More like, I feel—less respect for her."

"Because the guy she's going to the Harvest Ball with is holding her hand? Frankly, I don't see where a little hand holding ever hurt anyone."

We ordered our sodas in silence and then carried them over to the only available table—the one across from the booth where Sandy and Benjy were sitting. As we inched our legs under the little square table, Josh threw off his sour mood; in fact, he became downright jovial. And loud. At least loud enough to turn our neighbors' heads.

We all smiled and said, "Hi" pleasantly enough. But I felt tensions in the air. Some of them were mine.

I was drinking the last few drops of my Seven-Up when a small commotion sounded over by the entrance door. Several girls had gone to greet someone. I should have guessed that someone would be Rob.

Seeing this, Josh shook his head. "Just because he drew that cartoon. Sometimes," he brooded, "I don't understand women at all."

What was I supposed to say? That there was a charisma about Rob Carney that had eluded the rest of us all these years?

"So the strip is National Young Cartoonist contest material," he continued. "Big deal."

"Part of the big deal," I reminded him, "is what I contributed."

"Well, yeah, of course. And you were very good, too. A lot better than some people we know." His gaze flew to Sandy, then back to me. "But I'm talking *cartooning*. The talent for drawing. And I say—"

"I'd rather not discuss it, Josh."

"You're right. Let's forget all that boring stuff." He took my hand in his and pinned me with a look from those hypnotic dark eyes. "Let's talk about *us*."

All at once there was Rob, clumping toward us. "Hi there," he said. "Can you make room for an old visual arts buddy?"

"Nope," Josh said. "This is a tiny table, meant only for two people."

I automatically slid over and looked around for an extra chair—just because.

But Sandy, suddenly all smiles, said, "Over here, Rob. We have plenty of room."

So there we all were. Josh and me, at our table—Benjy, Sandy, and Rob, crowded together at their small booth.

The three of them seemed to be enjoying

themselves, talking in low tones, laughing now and then, glancing our way.

Josh had apparently forgotten all about discussing us. He was too busy trying to ferret out what, if anything, was going on at Sandy's booth. "Hey," he whispered hoarsely behind his hand, "did I see Carney put his arm around her?"

I tried to look without seeming to look, which was tough. Still, I, too, had a sudden need to know. "Oh, just lightly," I reported back. "The way anybody puts an arm around a good friend." A *very* good friend.

Just then in came Vicki Sellers and headed for Rob's booth. She murmured a few words, and Benjy slid over. Vicki crowded in and stared directly across at Rob.

Well, I'd pretty much had it. "Just to make sure everyone has enough room," I suggested to Josh, "why don't you and I take off? Then Rob and—and his little friend can have our whole table to themselves."

"Take off? Gladly," he said. He dumped our empty cups into the trash can, and we left.

I did glance back in time to see Vicki take over our table, then beckon to Rob to follow. I immediately wished I hadn't looked.

On the way home Josh sat behind the steering wheel wrapped in morose silence. And I was quieter than usual, as I worked up my nerve to bring up something I had been thinking about. "Josh," I ventured, watching his face for a reaction, "precisely why did you invite me to the Harvest Ball?"

"Why?" A tiny muscle flexed along his jawline. "Because I wanted to. Best reason in the world, wouldn't you say?"

"Did it have anything to do with what went wrong between you and Sandy?"

"Off limits," he said gruffly.

Another silence while I mulled that one over.

"OK, you want reasons? Try these on for size. For one, you're a good-looking girl, you know?"

"Gee, thanks."

"And you're not that tough to get along with. You're bright, but not show-off bright, and you're talented. Carney'd be the first to tell the world how great you are with ideas."

I'd explore that one later. I let him talk.

"Let's just say, you're the best of the lot. By far."

Romantic, right? But with the Harvest

Ball coming up in two days, I'd learn to live with it.

Later that night, while burrowed in the warmth of my bed, I remembered what Josh had said, "Carney'd be the first to tell the world . . ."

Rob and I quietly slipped "Windy Walpole" into Mr. Baldwin's desk drawer first thing Friday morning, then went on our ways. In class that day he announced—with pride in his voice—that our project would be the school's entry in the National Young Cartoonist contest. It was a great moment for Rob and me. Not all of the moments following it were destined to be that great.

That afternoon when school let out, I wasn't sure what to do with myself. I felt a little lost without Windy and Rob—as if I were rattling around inside a vacuum. Vacuums are really not my style.

But a new thought hit me. Why couldn't I wander down to the gym and see if I could help Rob out with the decorations? After all, I had been the other half of Carney and Marsh. The "idea" half. I headed down the hallway.

The gym had undergone quite a transformation already. Off to one side an oversized Styrofoam harvest moon was hemmed in by a bevy of potted scotch pines; the area was made more woodsy by the addition of some artificial grass and bushes. In the middle of these was placed a rustic bench. Giant aluminum stars winked in the "sky." The overhead lighting was mellow, bathing everything below in "moonlight." Along one wall they'd built a horse corral, and perched on the gate was the cardboard figure of a spindly male resembling Windy Walpole as a cowhand.

Anne Thomas spotted me and ambled over. "What do you think, Betsy? Not bad, huh?"

I searched for words and came up with a weak, "Very nice." I repeated it with more gusto. "*Very* nice!" Well, it was.

"And how do you like our little friend Windy on the corral gate? Nice touch, wouldn't you say?"

How could I deny it?

"That was my idea," Anne announced, beaming. "And Rob's construction. He really felt funny about it. Said the other kids would think he'd developed delusions of his own importance. And he thought he should

105

consult with you, since you'd been partners and all. But I persuaded him you'd love it."

"Right!" What *else* could I say?

From the corner of my eye, I could see Rob pause in his labors and glance our way.

"And to make it even more realistic," Anne went on, "a couple of girls have volunteered to do the little man in papier-mâché. Windy Walpole in three dimensions. Doesn't that sound neat?"

Rob had made it over to us. Anne greeted him with a hug, then linked her arm through his arm and turned that lovely face up to his. "Didn't I tell you Betsy wouldn't mind?"

Did I actually expect Rob to pull away from all of that? I mean, what guy would? So he did get a little red around the ears. Attention from a girl like Anne Thomas had to stir up all sorts of yearnings inside him.

"I hear you're going to the ball with Josh Amberston," Anne said. "Nice choice."

"And you?"

"I'm going with Hank Lowe. Good old Hank." She could have used that tone to describe her faithful dog or her pet frog. It was obvious she had used that tone of voice for Rob's benefit. It didn't take a massive intellect to realize she was thinking seductive little thoughts.

Still, why should it matter? Rob and I were reaching the end of our partnership. Only the results of the contest remained to keep us in any kind of contact. Very soon he'd go his way, I'd go mine. It was inevitable. As they say—life. And there was absolutely no point in feeling down about it. No point at all.

By the time I got home, I was feeling better—at least, more reconciled to my situation. Able to eat dinner, almost able to concentrate on my homework assignments.

Upstairs in my bedroom, I worked on math until the numbers began to jangle in my brain. Then I dug out the romance I'd been reading and tried to pick up where I'd left off. But all that stuff about love—as in kissing, holding someone tenderly, whispering into shell-pink ears—I mean, who was kidding whom? In *real* life the right guy didn't necessarily end up with the right girl. I closed the book.

The evening was moving along very slowly. Not that I didn't have several things to accomplish, such as laying out my clothes for the dance, shampooing my hair and trying out a color rinse I'd threatened so often to use. Or doing something about my ragged nails.

The phone rang beyond my door. I didn't bother to get up.

"Betsy!" Teddy hollered up the stairs. "It's for you."

"Who is it?" I mean, I wasn't about to get up for just *any*body.

Teddy paused about three seconds, then yelled, "I think it's Rob."

I galloped to the upstairs hall phone. Just as my fingers reached for the receiver, Teddy's voice returned from downstairs. "Or—was it Josh?"

It was Josh, of course. I kept the conversation brief and to the point, just in case someone else might happen to call.

Someone else did. Sandy rambled on for an endless half hour, talking about Benjy mostly—never even mentioning Josh. There were definite undercurrents that even my fogged-up brain could pick up. Later, the more rational part of my brain would play with the bits and pieces of the complicated Sandy-Josh business, then sort them out. And some of my confusion would be cleared up.

"By the way," Sandy said just before saying goodbye, "that partner of yours—is he a riot!"

I let that dangle for maybe a second. Then, "Oh?"

"I swear I laughed so hard last night my sides hurt. And Vicki Sellers is pretty amusing, too. I mean, talk about funny!"

If it was so funny, why wasn't I laughing?

After Sandy hung up, I checked myself out in the dresser mirror. Nothing very impressive stared back.

As I shampooed my hair, I debated the wisdom of using a color rinse and thought, *Why not?* The next morning, for sure. After that I sifted through the beauty-tips section of a magazine for a more interesting way to style my hair. Anything different would do.

Chapter Eight

The color rinse I used on my hair was a disaster. It in no way resembled the shade shown on the outside of the box. Strawberry blond, it said. But what came through was this peculiar shade that resembled a shiny new penny.

I read the fine print of the no-name brand instructions: "In four weeks, reapply." Did it mean I had to wait *four weeks* to get rid of that horrendous color?

Mom wasn't much help. For one thing, she was in the midst of planning for our family's annual Thanksgiving get-together. Her mind was on other things. She did take off enough time to let out a shriek when she saw me and say, "Betsy Marsh, what have you *done* to yourself?"

I explained, using as few words as possible.

"A no-name brand? Well, that says it right there. Companies who make no-name brands are not known for their careful labeling. And their guarantees are probably worthless. Oh, I suppose you could write to the company and complain—"

"Mother," I said, "the Harvest Ball is tonight. That means I need a miracle solution *today*."

"Well, I'm sorry, dear, I have no miracle solution. You could try washing your hair several times in a row, and it just might—"

"I've already tried that. And *look* at me."

I called up Sandy.

"The color of a new penny," she repeated after me. "Aren't you exaggerating just a little?"

"Come on over and see for yourself," I said.

I'd covered the whole mess with a loose kerchief and was trying to work my way through an early lunch, despite this huge knot in my stomach, when she got there.

I pushed back from the table and removed the kerchief.

"Wow!" Sandy surveyed me and pursed her lips. "You weren't exaggerating."

"Exactly. And I've got to get rid of it, somehow, before tonight. Listen, as a last resort, I'd even consider renting a wig. Yeah. Something in medium blond, with soft curls at the sides, and maybe a half-bang. Or—"

"Turn around," Sandy cut in.

I stared at her.

"Around," she said. "And around again." She watched carefully as I made a slow circle, then an about-face. "Hey," she said. "I wonder—"

"You're not the only one. Can you imagine me showing up at the ball looking like"—I picked up a strand of my hair and wiggled it—"*this*?"

"Easily," she said. And then, "Oh, sure, it probably should be toned down a little. But I don't think that's a problem. The shade is actually quite attractive with your coloring. That, and some styling—and, Betsy, old pal, we might just have something here."

"If you can pull this off," I said, "you're

definitely a miracle worker. And when it comes to favors, I'll owe you one."

Joanne arrived halfway through the new rinse to tone down the first one. For a couple of minutes she just sat back and watched. After that, questions and suggestions flew back and forth between her and Sandy. And suddenly my hair was the project of the week.

I ended up with a loose wave and a shorter cut, which just brushed my shoulders. The toned-down color didn't look half bad, a kind of chestnut. "It will go just great with that blue dress." Sandy was enthusiastic. "The style fits your face perfectly."

"Doesn't exactly resemble the kid sister I remember," Joanne commented dryly. "But that's all right. She could stand the change. Although," she added, "it's just too bad this whole glorious experiment will be wasted on Josh Amberston."

Sandy reared back as if someone had just stepped on her toe. "Uh, precisely what do you mean by that?"

"It's certainly no secret, Sandy, that Betsy and Josh are not what you'd call a couple made in heaven." Pause. Then, "I'm surprised you're still interested enough in the guy to ask."

"I'm—I'm not. It's just that I—we—" A redness had taken over Sandy's cheeks. She suddenly became very busy with my "chestnut" hair. "Why don't we try a soft curl here? Like this. What do you think, Joanne?"

Joanne and I exchanged a quick glance. A lot went into that glance. Bits of knowledge that had suddenly come together, like troublesome jigsaw-puzzle pieces. And just maybe the beginnings of a plan. "Very nice, Sandy," Joanne said brightly. "And we could also try—" They were back in the hairstyling business.

"All right," Joanne said, "so now we know. She's still got a thing for Josh." My sister and I were sitting around that Saturday afternoon comparing notes. I was sitting without moving, so as not to disturb my nest of carefully constructed curls. Joanne, who was going nowhere special, was sprawled on the sofa, cutting her toenails. She paused in her labors. "But," she said, "can anything positive really come of it? Of course, if Josh felt something special for *her*—"

"Actually," I thought aloud, "I'm not sure he doesn't." My mind furiously pieced together certain events of the past several weeks. In particular, I couldn't forget Josh's reaction to Sandy and Benjy that night at BurgerMaster.

"But the fact is that Sandy will be there with Benjy, even though she's probably dying to go out with Josh. And since I'll be there with Josh—"

"And you're dying to go with Rob—"

Charged silence.

"All right," Joanne said, folding up her clippers and swinging to her feet, "don't admit it out loud. But think about what I've said. Am I even a little right?" She pointed a finger at me, without waiting for me to answer. "Maybe you'll get your own act together and do something about it."

After Joanne left the room, I kept sitting there, guarding my new hairstyle and thinking.

The evening started out the way such evenings should, with a lovely orchid corsage pinned on by my date—who, by the way, looked pretty gorgeous himself. Josh liked my hair, I guess. At least, he kept staring at it and smiling. And he liked my gown—even though it *wasn't* fuchsia.

We even lucked out on the weather. It was one of those crisp, clear nights, with a velvet sky filled with stars and a sliver of a moon.

Even the ride to Summerfield High was pleasant—soft FM music, with Josh singing along in his really good bass voice. Almost irresistible.

In the school parking lot I sat comfortably close to Josh and waited for him to remove the key from the ignition. He was staring through the window on his side as if caught up in a trance. Then, suddenly, he leaned toward me and cupped my hands in his and said, "You look good enough to eat," bringing his face next to mine.

For one brief instant I wondered if I'd read his feeling about Sandy correctly. And then I saw what he'd just seen—Sandy, looking like a doll in her emerald green formal, walking daintily along the parking lot with Benjy Marmon holding her elbow as if it were fragile china.

I didn't see any point in sitting there like a silent lump. So I opened my window and hollered, "Hi, Sandy! Hi, Benjy! How about waiting up for us?" I considered it a sign of gross immaturity for Josh to thump his forehead against the steering wheel and mutter curse words under his breath.

Sandy glanced up, looked somewhat startled, and obediently slowed her pace; Benjy smiled and waved and kept his other hand protectively at her elbow.

I hopped out of the car and headed toward them, forcing Josh to get out and stumble after me.

The four of us made it to the school entrance more or less together. Benjy and I did most of the talking; the other two uttered sounds. But mumbles and grunts do not a conversation make.

Some of the rooms on the first floor had been left open, reserved for hanging up coats and stuff. Our visual arts room was one of them. While the guys acted gallant and took care of our coats, Sandy and I hung around just outside the gym and exchanged guarded glances.

"That emerald green is definitely your color," I finally said.

"Your hair looks just great," she said. "Got to say I did a pretty good job."

There was another small silence while Sandy and I groped for more small talk.

"Benjy looks great all dressed up like that. It's fun to see all the guys dressed for a change," I said.

"True," Sandy said. "And Josh looks—nice, too."

Nothing ventured, nothing gained. I took the plunge. "Can I ask you something, well, important?"

"I guess so."

"About you and Josh. I detect definite signs of interest there. He leaves whiffs of it every time your name is mentioned. And you—"

"Let's go," Benjy said to Sandy. He looked all set to get the evening going.

Well, I'd talk to Sandy later. One way or another, I'd get her and Josh back on the right track. Just then, Josh came over, and he and I followed Sandy and Benjy to the gym.

The gym looked even more spectacular than it had when I had seen it the day before. And on the corral fence our Windy Walpole

118

looked achingly alive in papier-mâché as he straddled the gate.

"I love it," Sandy said the words. I echoed them in my mind.

Rob's subtle touch was everywhere. In the clustering of the scotch pines, in the efficient placing of the eight-piece dance band, in the air of playfulness and warmth, combined with just enough formality to tie the whole thing together. Exactly right for the Harvest Ball.

"I wonder where our cartoonist genius is tonight," Sandy mused. "He does plan on coming, right? Still coming by himself? Or did Rosemary Teal finally convince him—"

"By himself," I cut in quickly.

In a side room that joined the gym by a door, the refreshment committee had set up long dining tables and loaded them with platters of cold cuts, sliced turkey, meatballs in gravy, several types of salads, baked beans, molded whipped Jello-O—just about everything.

Josh and I went over to the punch bowl first. Sandy, with Benjy still in tow, was hovering over the meatballs, apparently trying to decide whether eating a few of them was worth the extra strain on the snug waistline of her formal. She settled for two. I started with good intentions, planning on the punch, maybe a little salad, a slice or two of turkey. And then my fork reached out and speared some ham, dinner rolls, and several slices of turkey.

And I'd have eaten it all, too, except—

"Say, guess who just came in," Sandy mumbled through mouthful of potato chips. "Your pal and mine, Rob Carney, surrounded by a whole harem of beauties." She craned her neck. "My oh my, what has the boy done to himself?"

I almost didn't recognize him. I mean, Rob, outfitted in a *tux*? Perfectly fitting jacket, black pants and vest, chalk-white shirt, black bow tie? Come *on*. It took several glances before my old brain absorbed that one.

My fingers strayed to the potato chips, grabbed a generous handful, then stuffed them into my mouth. I chewed slowly while I surveyed the wonder that was Rob.

"And his hair," Sandy half-whispered, poking me. "Can you believe that?"

It was neatly combed, with the familiar chestnut cowlick tamed at last—or beaten into submission. For a second a part of me missed that unruly mane he'd called his hair. Then sanity returned. "He certainly looks presentable," I said. "And it's about time."

"The guy actually looks civilized," Josh muttered. "It's enough to make you believe in miracles and the tooth fairy all over again."

Rob had attracted a cluster of girls. Anne Thomas was the one physically closest to him; she'd managed, somehow, to link her arm through his, leaving poor Hank Lowe to sulk in his corner and think dark thoughts.

And of course there was good old Rosemary Teal, who had decided to come to the dance by herself. She'd planted herself on the other side of Rob, looking right at home there. Anyone could see she was still nurturing hopes.

Rob moved slowly from the doorway to the food tables, still trailed by a couple of his fans. He caught my eye. "Hi, partner," he said. "Love the hair." And then he smiled.

Rob's teeth are very white. And when he smiles, his whole face lights up. Why hadn't I realized before the charm of his smile?

Josh, looking less than pleased, grabbed hold of my arm, almost spilling my punch,

121

and steered me to one of the tables lining the walls. We sat down and began to eat.

After a while Josh quit eating and looked up to watch me pick through my salad. "What's the matter?"

"I—I guess I'm not as hungry as I thought I was." Not much of an answer. But it would have to do until I'd worked out answers to—certain other questions. I could hear Joanne's voice ringing in my ears: "Don't admit it out loud. . . . Am I even a little right?" The feast on my plate just sat there.

Sandy and Benjy sat at another table, near the refreshments. Nothing seemed to be ruining *her* appetite. I watched as Sandy went back for seconds and then thirds; she usually eats when something's bothering her.

Rosemary had pretty much corralled Rob for herself. They stood together, balancing their plates in their hands. After a decent interval, she talked him into putting down their plates and going onto the dance floor.

"This ought to provide some entertainment." Josh did some snickering of his own. "The last time I saw Carney on the dance floor, he got all tangled up in his partner's feet. In fact," he added, "since you're not going to eat anyway, why don't we wander into the gym and observe the klutz in living color?"

The beat of the music was lively. I talked Josh into waiting for a slower song, so we just stood by and watched.

We watched Rob and Rosemary. Rob was dancing surprisingly well.

"I guess he's practiced since last time," Josh decided rather glumly.

"I guess." But who'd been teaching him? Rosemary? Vicki? Or—?

"Hey, the beat's changing," Josh reported. "Let's get in on this one."

So there we were, Josh and I, gliding across the dance floor. Together. My face was pressed against his shoulder, his arm encircled me, holding me close. It was just the way I'd always pictured it.

Not that far from us, Sandy and Benjy were doing their best to resemble a couple enjoying themselves. In reality they looked like two robots dancing together. You could actually see Benjy's lips move as he counted in time to the beat. Every now and then Sandy would glance over at Josh and me. I knew there was pain behind those big blue eyes.

Well, it wasn't as if I really wanted it this

way. If I could have figured out a civilized way to wish Josh off my back, Sandy would be welcome to him, no questions asked.

And that feeling grew while we were sitting out a dance. For one thing, Josh had gone back to his nasty remarks about "Windy Walpole." Every time his gaze settled on the papier-mâché figure, he made some nasty remark.

"Listen," he said, "I'm not criticizing your work on the project. The text was great. What I think stinks is the cartooning."

"Stinks?" I sat up straight. "Rob's work *stinks*?" I drew in a sharp breath. "No way!"

"Hey, take it easy," he said, waving me back. "I just told you, nothing personal intended. It's Carney's talent I'm questioning, remember?"

"Keep it to yourself, Amberston," I said. "When you insult Rob Carney, you insult—" *Me*? Was that what I was about to blurt out?

"Well, I must say I admire your loyalty to the guy. I could have stood a little loyalty from my partner, a couple of weeks ago. Boy, she really made me mad. Called my drawings of 'Bo McClure' 'crude.' Can you believe it? And it all started just because I suggested that her ideas for the strip weren't quite sharp enough. I put it as gently as I could. But, man, did she ever get mad! After that—" Josh stirred in his chair and examined his fingernails. "Maybe I should've kept my mouth shut, huh? Maybe if I hadn't pointed out where she went wrong, she wouldn't have said—" He slumped forward. "Ah, who cares?"

Josh Amberston did. Definitely. Even though he was too proud to admit it.

Rob waltzed over and held out his hands. "Hi, partner. How's about a dance with an old pal?"

That devastating smile again.

"Don't stick around on my account," Josh said. "It wouldn't be bad for me to just sit here awhile and do the thinking I should have done a couple of weeks ago."

Rob and I were in the middle of the floor, swaying together to the rhythm of a romantic slow tune when he asked, "What's bothering Josh?"

"Nothing he wouldn't be able to change with a few kind words in a certain person's direction," I said.

Rob's arm tightened about me. I rested my cheek against the black vest. His heart thumped reassuringly through it. I could hear him humming along with the band—off-key, as usual. But so what? It sounded like Rob and was as natural as river water slapping against rocks.

"This is really fun," Rob murmured against my hair. "You and me dancing without a big fight brewing. I like it this way."

Me, too, Rob. Me, too.

"Lots of the praise I've been hearing about 'Windy' has been meant for you," he said. "I keep telling everybody what a great job you did. And how much the success of our strip is because of your plotting."

"Thanks, friend," I said.

"Friendship," he said. "That's what it's all about with us. Right?" He zigged, then zagged, bringing us back to the middle of the floor. "Liking. Respecting. Being comfortable with each other. The basis for any real friendship. Agreed?"

"Well—I guess."

He changed position, holding me at a slight distance. "I suppose it's even possible that all those years I was making a pest of myself, following you around, what I was really looking for was just a pal to hang out with."

Me?

The music stopped as the band paused between numbers. Rob and I stayed put, with most of the other couples, and waited.

"At least, that's Rosemary's theory," he kept on talking. "Although I think she's stretching a point. I can't quite believe—Hi, Rosemary. What's up?"

That girl had actually come into the middle of the dance floor, taken Rob's arm from me, turned him around, and said loudly enough for several people to hear, "You promised the next dance to me, remember?"

"What? I promised . . .?" He yanked at a stray lock of his hair. "Yeah, I guess I did. But—" His eyes met mine, then glanced away. "I promised. What can I say?"

"Here comes Josh," Rosemary volunteered. She grabbed Rob's wrist and tugged. "Come on, Rob."

He went with her. No argument, no backward glance, not even a dragging step.

Well, there it was. When I'd finally come to terms with my true feelings for Rob, he felt differently about me. Where did I go from here?

Josh approached me, and we stayed there, going through the motions of dancing until the band took a break. Then Josh suddenly came to life. "I've been doing some thinking," he said. "About Rob's cartooning and mine." He rubbed his chin. "I couldn't be all that crude, and he couldn't be all that perfect. There's just no way that could happen."

A sore loser, Sandy had called him. Totally unable to admit he could be wrong.

"Tell you what," he said. "Let's go into visual arts and check out Rob's cartoons. I know where they are. In the bottom drawer in Baldwin's desk."

"That's really a dumb idea. You've seen his drawings over and over. You know exactly what they're like."

He grabbed my hand. "Please, Betsy. I've got to see them again without lots of people around. I've got to study them and prove something to myself, once and for all."

We got to visual arts just as a couple of girls were leaving the room.

"Let's make this quick," I snapped out. "And please treat those panels carefully."

"Not to worry," Josh said cheerfully. "All I want to do is prove to myself that his cartoons aren't better than mine."

Well, maybe he'd be able to finally see the

difference between mediocre and excellent. And maybe he'd finally stop bugging me and everyone else.

He pulled the desk drawer open. Sure enough, there was our accordian-pleated folder right on top.

I could see that he was tense. His fingers trembled as he loosened the elastic cord that bound the folder. He reached in, grabbed a bunch of the panels, and yanked them out.

No, not quite out. The corners of several panels had gotten caught inside the folder.

"Watch it, Amberston," I muttered. "You'll rip—"

I heard the tearing noise. He'd done it. Just like *that*. Ripped the series of panels into jagged twos.

Josh let out a sharp cry, then just stared, mouth open, for a few moments. "I can't believe I did this," he finally said in a muffled voice. "Never in a million years would I deliberately—"

Part of me believed him and felt sorry for him. But the rest of me wanted to scream and kick at Josh. I felt as if I, too, had been wounded by his careless hand.

I knew what I had to do: get ahold of Rob,

haul him into visual arts, and let him see for himself. Then I would find myself a quiet corner, slip into it, and cry. . . .

Rob was struggling hard to take it well. "These—these things sometimes happen." He flicked through some of the sheets. He inhaled and held his breath. The exhale was kind of noisy. "It may take a little repair work, here and there."

"A little?" Josh exclaimed. "Man, do you realize what I just did here? I destroyed six weeks of really professional work! And for what?"

Sandy was there, too, perched as near to Josh as she could get without ending up in his lap. She'd left Benjy standing in the middle of the dance floor to follow us to the visual arts room. And she obviously meant to stay put, no matter what. Josh seemed glad to have her around.

"We still have a little over a week until the official turn-in time," Rob said. "If Betsy and I get right at it—"

"You've got eight days, at the outside. If you count Thanksgiving." Then Josh suddenly brightened. "But, hey, Carney, I can help you. I'm pretty good at inking in, even if my cartoons do reek."

"Josh Amberston," Sandy said, "your cartoons in no way reek. And I never want to hear you down on yourself again. Got me?"

"Gotcha." And then, "The offer's an honest one, Rob. I—that is, Sandy and I—"

"The way I see it," Rob cut back in, "Betsy and I started Windy Walpole when he was a few scrawls on my sketch pad. What I'm trying to say is, it was Betsy and me in the beginning, and it only seems right that it's just the two of us in the end."

End. What a terribly final word.

We wandered back to the Harvest Ball after deciding we'd rest on Sunday and tackle the cartoons fresh on Monday. Rosemary reshackled Rob and hung onto him, laughing and chattering as if they were an actual couple. She did her best to keep him out of my view. Josh dutifully escorted me through the rest of the evening, but I didn't need a whack across the head to know where his true interest lay. I'd seen him whisper something to Sandy just before she rejoined Benjy, and I'd seen those big blue eyes light up.

To be truthful, I was glad for both of them.

It seemed only right that something good should come out of what had turned into a disastrous evening.

I stayed awake well into the morning hours going over in my mind the details of that long night. Thinking about what I'd said to Rob, what Rob had said to me. And one word stuck around to torment me: *end*.

Should I have caught on sooner? Had the signals been pointing to it all along? Had the lively beginnings of Carney and Marsh dwindled through lack of nourishment to an inevitable end?

Well, I had no one but myself to blame for that.

Chapter Nine

On Monday morning there was quite a scene.

"Josh Amberston, you did *what*?" Mr. Baldwin screamed as he leaned over the desk.

Josh backed up a pace or two. "Well, uh, I didn't—I didn't *deliberately*—"

"You mean, it was an accident that your hand found that desk drawer, slipped in, pulled out, and ruined the best thing to happen to this class in a decade?"

Just four of us—Josh, Sandy, Rob and me—were in visual arts extra-early that morning. And when Mr. Baldwin's voice rose and hit a high note, Sandy moved in on Josh as if to protect him with her nearness.

I could see Josh turn red as he struggled with words. There weren't too many that he could make sound convincing. And Mr. Baldwin was in no mood to let him off the hook.

"It's OK, Mr. Baldwin," Rob said. "Betsy and I have the situation in hand. We're going to work on the panels over the next few days and whip them back into shape."

Mr. Baldwin held out several sheets. "Do you realize the condition these are in? In no way repairable."

"Then we'll do them over completely."

"It'll take time—"

"Betsy and I have the time over vacation. We can work at one of our houses. We'll get them done."

"You picked a great time to ask for working space around here," my mother said apologetically. "You know it'll be a problem with the preparations for Thanksgiving. I feel terrible that I can't help more."

The only available space would be our glassed-in back porch, where the only source of heat consists of an ancient wood stove. Still, it was better than nothing.

We worked intensely all Monday afternoon

134

and evening. Mom saw to it that nobody wandered out to distract us. It was a very productive time.

Isn't it odd how you can sometimes look into a face that's as familiar as an old childhood doll's and suddenly see a different person there? That's how it was when, between heavy spells of inking, I sneaked glances at Rob.

Remarkable things happened, during those glances. Take Rob's nose, for instance. Why had I never noticed how neatly it fit in with those really good cheekbones and deepset blue eyes? And Rob's hands—beautifully shaped, with strong fingers that moved with precision and grace. And his forearms, with the tiny golden hairs glistening like silk beneath the lamplight. And the whole lean look of him as he strained forward over the card table and performed his magic with the figure of Rosalie.

He caught me peering at him and smiled self-consciously. "What's the matter? Is there ink on my face or something?"

"Uh, in a way," I fibbed. "There's this little—speck, right here on your cheek." I lifted a hand to brush off the imaginary what-

135

ever. My fingers met his face and tingled as if there were an electric current flowing between us.

"Got it?" I noticed his whitened knuckles, when he massaged his kneecap through the denim of his jeans.

I thought it must be that my touch was irritating him. After all, we'd gotten together for one reason: to repair the damage to "Windy Walpole," thereby bringing the whole episode to a final, definite end.

Joanne pounced on me as soon as Rob took off. "Well? What happened?"

"We inked in one three-paneled strip and got started on another."

"Come *on*, Betsy, give me a break. I'm talking romance. Rob. Progress."

"I don't know what you're yakking about," I said, trying to keep cool. "It was business. Purely business."

"Not exactly the way you had it planned, if I've read little sister right."

I really shouldn't have let Joanne get to me. I shouldn't have shouted at her. I shouldn't have said what I did. But the painful fact was, Joanne had hit the proverbial nail square on the head. I, who had jeered at and complained about Rob for so long, had finally stumbled into love with him just as he had sidestepped out of love with me.

Sometimes people enjoy ganging up on me. Joanne and Sandy made an afternoon of it on Tuesday.

Joanne was waiting for me in the living room when I got home. "Considering the closeness of you two old buddies," she said, putting on that wise smile she saves for these occasions, "the least Rob could have done was walk you home."

"He's coming over at four," I said defensively.

"That's not good enough. I expect more than a working relationship here. After all these years of hovering around little sister, Rob owes this family—"

"Rob owes this family *nothing*," I snapped back, and I would have said much more, but the sudden sting behind my eyelids warded me off.

Oh, I knew she was only making her little joke. She liked Rob, and she hoped for more for us. She'd probably guessed the pain I was feeling and was trying to kid me out of it.

Shortly after that Sandy arrived—a brand-new version of Sandy, rosy and glowing. Mr. Right had done wonders.

What is there about people in love that makes them want to convert the whole world into matched sets? I tried to explain to Sandy that not everyone can be so lucky. Some of us are destined to go on for years, alone and struggling.

"You don't know what you're saying, Betsy," she insisted. "I know the signs, and I'm telling you, do not count Rob Carney out. That whole dumb business with Rosemary Teal is nothing to worry about. I mean the girl is just pushy, and Rob hasn't figured out how to brush her off. But you can bet—"

"I'd rather not," I interrupted. "My luck just isn't good enough these days."

"Gosh, how did it get so late; I really can't stick around," Sandy said, looking at our clock. "I told Josh I'd meet him at Burger-Master by four. Please, Betsy, don't give up on Rob."

Rob arrived promptly at four and immediately went in to add a couple of logs to the wood stove. I got some glazed doughnuts from the pantry and fixed two cups of hot chocolate, and we settled in for the rest of the afternoon.

Most of the time I worked intently on the Sunday strip, inking in and tinting. But once in a while I'd sneak a glimpse of Rob. And once I actually dropped everything just to sit there and stare at him. But he didn't seem to notice—or at least, he didn't catch my eye.

Shortly after five the phone rang. It was for Rob, Joanne announced all twinkly-eyed. And guess who'd gone to all the trouble of tracking him down at our house? Rosemary.

A few unbearably long minutes passed as Rob talked on the phone, and I chewed on the end of my pen and thought nasty little thoughts until his return.

"That Rosemary," Rob said, shaking his head and reseating himself at the card table. "She never knows when to lay off."

"Oh?" I said, waiting for the rest of the tale about Rosemary. But Rob had already slipped back into the work.

At five-fifteen Mom cut all action short with her arrival and an announcement of her own. She was apologetic and half-unnerved by a phone call *she'd* received. It appeared that we Marshes were about to inherit her younger brother, Frank, his wife, and their three sons for Thanksgiving. They'd decided to take the boys out of school early to be able to spend several days with us, starting that very evening. "And I asked myself," she went on, " 'where can I put those live wire boys where they won't disrupt the whole household?' I have to put the boys up out here on the porch, in those fold-away cots stored in the attic."

"Which leaves us with no place to finish the strips," I said.

"And, Betsy, I'm really going to need some help, so if you could postpone work on the cartooning until the day after Thanksgiving. It was lucky they gave you tomorrow off, too, for that teachers meeting."

"But, Mom! Our *deadline*—"

Rob's voice boomed in, "Hey, no sweat." His smile radiated total confidence. "We'll finish up at my house, Friday afternoon and Saturday morning. We're that near to being done."

Friday and Saturday. And then it would be the end for Carney and Marsh?

I watched Rob stack our papers and carefully place them into the accordian-pleated folder. He dug out his gloves, turned up the collar of his fur-lined jacket, waved goodbye at the door, and then he was gone. I wouldn't be seeing him for two whole days.

It's just as well that pre-Thanksgiving preparations around our house don't leave much time for brooding. My mother has a real talent for assigning chores. She ordered me to dust and vacuum downstairs, sticking Joanne with the entire upstairs. Teddy was handed the silver polish, then set before a drawerful of tarnished knives, forks, and spoons and told to go to it. Even Dad, who's a master evader, was talked into rearranging furniture and bringing firewood to the glassed-in porch.

And then, right after the evening news, in trooped Uncle Frank, Aunt Vivian, and their three sons.

Mom prefers to call my cousins "live wires." I have more descriptive names for them. The politest one is not polite enough to utter aloud. Just let it be said that over the course of three days with Frank Jr., Danny, and little Kevin, I found it very hard to resist the urge to strangle them.

And, of course, Aunt Vivian, who never

lets anything go unspoken, had to mention my hair. "My goodness," she said, "what happened to Betsy's beautiful blond hair? That color looks positively *awful*."

To my surprise Mom came to my defense. "Actually, Vivian," she said, "that color is very 'in' this season. It's such a warm brown, and Betsy's received many compliments because of it." She eyed Aunt Vivian and said, "I must say I'm surprised that you didn't know."

That was one of the few bright spots in the whole blah holiday period.

Thanksgiving Day brought out both sets of grandparents, uncles, aunts, and cousins enough to start a rough-and-tumble football game in the backyard. We played until it began to snow. Then we ended up inside the house, reduced to squabbling over Monopoly, endless card games, and TV program choices.

Our dining table was stretched with leaves, to fit sixteen, and a smaller table was set up for the little kids. There was plenty of everything. The turkey disappeared in a record thirty-five minutes, leaving behind the usual bare bones. Grandparents, uncles, aunts, cousins all yakked and giggled and argued and reminisced. Then Dad dragged out the slides and home movies, and we sat on the living room floor in clusters and watched the family history flash past.

Everybody had a great time, I guess. As for me—well, I did have this headache; and along about the middle of the home movies, I developed an almost overwhelming desire to sneak into my bedroom, close the door, and cry.

There were a few stares and raised brows in my direction, so it must have showed. I overheard Grandma Wentworth approach Mom with, "Grace, what in the world is wrong with Betsy? She seems so—I don't know. Not her normal sunny self."

And Mom said, "She's sixteen. Need I say more?"

From the suddenly wise expression on Grandma Wentworth's face, I got the feeling that all her questions had just been answered. I resented that. All troubles and conditions couldn't possibly boil down to the fact that I was sixteen.

Most of the relatives had taken off for home by eight that evening. Only Uncle Frank and his family remained, but I had no intention of sticking around to collect insults or trade kicks and slaps with the likes of Frank Jr., Danny, and Kevin.

My darkened bedroom felt deliciously warm and safe from prying eyes. And when I eased myself between the sheets and buried my face in the pillow, I tried to blank everything from my mind.

It almost worked, except for Rob's familiar image, which kept bobbing up on the grayed-out screen behind my eyes.

Suddenly a phone sounded far away, but I kept my eyes closed.

I lay there half asleep until Joanne burst into the room. "Hey, guess who's on the phone?"

I mumbled something and turned my face to the pillow.

"It's Windy Walpole himself, asking for you."

Naturally I opened my eyes.

"Windy, otherwise known as Rob."

That got me up all right. And I could hear Joanne's laughter floating behind me, all the way to the phone.

"Hi," Rob said. Pause. Then, "Had a good day?"

"Oh—a busy one."

"Know what you mean. Man, did we have relatives! Must have been two million of them. But they're gone now. Free at last."

A silence. To fill it up, we both began talking at once. "You're still coming over here tomorrow?" Rob asked a little cautiously. Wasn't I supposed to say yes?

"I certainly plan to. If," I added, for insurance, "it's OK with your mother."

"Oh, *sure*. I mean, she's looking forward to—well, watching us finish up the 'Windy' panels."

Finish up. A neat way to put it.

The conversation dwindled after that to "What time tomorrow?" from me, and "How about ten-thirty in the morning?" from Rob.

Not much material there to dream on. . . .

Rob's mother didn't exactly hover, but she did flutter around a lot—delivering a plate of brownies, following them up with chocolate milk, a couple of oranges, and something she called apricot surprise, which she insisted was terribly nutritious. At last she ran out of things to flutter about, and we got down to business.

We worked right through lunch, with five

145

minutes off to digest some blended stuff Mrs. Carney had made up, then five more minutes to stretch and work the stiffness from our fingers. "Windy Walpole" was moving right along. No doubt we'd finish that very afternoon. Which would make Saturday—all day, Saturday—a day off. Or, as Rob might put it, we'd be free at last.

"Boy, this Sunday strip is really something," Rob remarked. He dabbed a smidgeon of nut brown to Rosalie's long hair, then held up the panel and smiled at the delicate face. "Aah, the lovely Rosalie. Never argues, never bosses, never runs around on her guy." He blew the panel a kiss. "Rosalie," he said, "my best girl."

I'd been working on Hannah, leaving the others to Rob. He'd been working doubly hard on Rosalie, apparently having problems. From the corner of my eye, I'd seen him discard several sheets in his quest for perfection. This last panel must have measured up.

We'd picked up an audience early in the game. Rob's sister, Kimberly, who'd been making wisecracks and nosing about, found the discards. She held one out to Rob. "Hey, look at this," she chirped. "I'll bet you I know who—"

Rob made a grab for the paper, wrinkling it rather badly. He flashed his sister a ferocious scowl. And when at last she left and the air cleared, we returned to the work at hand.

And suddenly that was *it*. We were finished.

Rob yawned and stretched, then glanced over at me. "Well, partner, we made it. Great feeling, huh?"

"Great," I agreed, keeping my voice hearty, feeling anything but great.

He brought out a brand-new folder and placed the panels into it with extreme care. Then he gathered up a batch of leftovers and crammed them in the accordian-pleated disaster. "Finally we can trash this mess. Although," he said, looking thoughtful, "in a way, it's too bad. A lot of work went into them. But—you know what they say. Off with the old, on with the new."

I'd never been happy with that particular saying. And the thought of trashing six precious weeks of Rob's and my efforts hurt in a special way.

For once Rob picked up my thoughts

remarkably well. "If you want them," he said, "they're yours." He added a couple of discards, using a little more care. "You can hang them up for the world to see. You can paper your walls, spread them on the bottom of a bird cage, stuff them into your wood stove. Whatever." He scribbled a makeshift seal on the outside of the folder, then held up his right hand, with palm out. "I hereby bequeath every gorgeous thing in here to the great Betsy Marsh."

He grinned. "Know something? We should celebrate. What do you say, we head for BurgerMaster?"

"Oh—I don't know." I didn't think I could take much more of his good-old-pal attitude.

"Come on. My treat."

"Well—"

And that's how we ended up at Burger-Master. Just Rob Carney and me, sitting across from each other like two regular buddies.

We were not alone. Sandy and Josh occupied a table across from us and waved hello before putting their heads together over ice-cream sodas. Behind us Rosemary Teal was turning her charms on Benjy Marmon.

Vicki Sellers was table hopping like mad. Anne Thomas had discovered Mike Hennessey and was deep in conversation with him. Altogether, a rare collection of friends and others.

"Makes you feel right at home, right?" Rob surveyed the busy scene. "Like the whole crowd's around."

"Yeah. And here comes one of them now." Dear little Vicki, with mouth already open, ready to sing out a greeting.

I grabbed the accordian-pleated folder, meaning to tuck it under my arm away from sight.

But nothing escapes the eyes of some people. "Oh, *there* it is! Rob's precious brainchild. Let's see!" And she reached out.

Rob's fingers caught her wrist and hung on. "No," he said, his voice sharper than I'd ever heard it. "That's Betsy's. She worked on it right along with me. And everything in that folder belongs to her."

"Well, OK." She shook off his fingers and gave him a frown. "Boy, Carney, you're just too much."

Rob stared at her, then focused in on his knuckles. "Goodbye, Vicki," he said. "See you around."

But Vicki had already glided off, searching for another table with another guy. One who was in the mood for her message.

Joanne was parked on the living room sofa when I got home. She'd practically tied herself to the phone and was trying to outshout Frank Jr., Danny, and Kevin, who were wrestling on the floor, with Teddy on the sidelines egging them on.

I needed peace, quiet, and space to spread out the contents of that beat-up folder. I wanted to relive our brighter moments and do some thinking. Even knowing that Rob and I would never be more than pals hadn't changed my feelings for him. Daydreaming was not a substitute for the real thing, but it certainly was better than nothing at all.

Joanne had finished her call. She motioned to me. "What's up?" She spotted the folder. "Aha! The gory remains of Windy the Great!"

She would give me no peace until I agreed to open the folder and lay out the tattered paperwork on the dining room table. Joanne caught it first. A single large, tinted panel in the center of a partially crumpled sheet. She held it out. "Our girl Rosalie?" Then she yanked it back and gave it the eagle eye. "Or—another girl we all know and love?"

"Let me see that!" I said as I reached for it.

But Joanne had a death grip on it. The sound coming out of her mouth was a laugh of pure delight, which drew the wrestling match to an abrupt halt and attracted a herd of spectators.

"Say," Teddy piped up, "isn't that Betsy?"

If I focused on the brown hair, the sprinkling of freckles at the bridge of the nose, the shape of the eyes, the set of the cleft chin it looked like me. "Rosalie." I could hear Rob's voice ringing in my ears. "My best girl."

"I would say," Joanne put it plainly, "that the boy is trying to tell you something."

I'd recognized the wrinkles at the bottom of the paper. Rob himself had contributed those when he snatched the sheet from Kimberly. And I remembered how he'd scowled at her when—

"If I were you," Joanne broke into my thoughts, "I'd grab that guy before somebody else beats you to it." She handed me the damaged panel. "I wouldn't begin to tell you how to go about it," she said, "but since you're the original idea girl, I know you'll find a way."

Find a way. The words repeated inside my head as I marched up the stairs to my room.

For a while I stood at my bedroom window, staring out at the graying sky. Rob's house was over there somewhere out of sight—a middle-sized, brown-shingled home surrounded by other middle-sized homes.

Had Rob intentionally drawn Rosalie to look like me, hoping I'd make the next move?

I hoped so and made a choice. I dug out my old note pad, uncapped a pen, and turned the radio on to some soft music. Then I planted myself before my desk and began to sort out my feelings by writing about Rosalie and her boyfriend, Ken, whom she'd known most of her life. I detailed Ken's fierce attempts to win her love and her even fiercer attempts to knock them flat. And I continued by writing that the day came when Rosalie awakened to her true feelings for the guy, only to suspect that his love had cooled down and that he was about to wander off—for good.

Rob would have no trouble recognizing himself. Or me. Or my message.

I worked on the story for a couple of hours—right up until dinner time. Then I dropped the pad and pen, inched onto my bed, and lay there with my eyes closed.

I had put everything I'd learned, and more, into that story line. It was as tight and right as I could make it. In a few minutes I would go downstairs and talk Teddy into delivering a long white envelope to the Carney house after dinner.

Chapter Ten

There is no way to guarantee privacy in our house. But I did my best by staying upstairs, away from the downstairs crowd, yet mere inches from the phone in the hall. I tried to look occupied, with my nose deep in a book. In no time the downstairs crowd became the upstairs intruders, clumping up the steps, arguing, shouting.

"You know what they say about that watched pot," Joanne cooed as she tiptoed past, smiling.

"The one that never boils?"

Another little smile.

I, for one, was getting pretty weary of moldy old sayings, wise smiles, and sisters who made a practice of hanging around underfoot. "Don't you have anything more exciting to do?"

"Lucky you," she said, "I'll be leaving as soon as Tony calls to say he's on the way." Tony was Joanne's latest boyfriend. Perhaps, if I was lucky, she'd get so distracted by him that she'd get off my case for a while.

Just then the phone rang, but I got to it first. "Yes?" I put a hand to my chest, to steady the thumping.

"Hi, this is Tony McMichaels, and I'm, uh, looking for Joanne."

At least it got her out of my hair.

Shortly after Joanne left, I heard the front door slam downstairs. Teddy was back from Rob's; his loud mouth gave him away.

Since I preferred not to bring the entire household into this, I had to wait patiently while Teddy bustled around the kitchen, getting himself a snack, before he finally made his way upstairs.

"Well?" I restrained myself from grabbing hold of Teddy and trying to shake the news out of him. "What happened?"

Teddy took his time answering. "Well,

Rob came to the door—" He took a noisy slurp from a can of ginger ale.

"Yeah? Come *on*, you dope. What did he say?"

"Dope?" He put down his ginger ale, then drew himself up and folded his arms across his chest. "I did not come up here to be insulted. Especially after I just did you a huge favor."

"Sorry about that, Ted. It's just that I—"

"OK. So let's see. He came to the door and I said, 'Betsy told me to give you this envelope.' And he said, 'Thanks, Teddy.' And I said, 'She's upstairs at home, sitting next to the phone.' And he said, 'I'll be calling her.' And I said, 'Goodbye.' And—and that's it."

Rob had told Teddy he would be phoning. I'd been sitting next to that instrument of torture for almost an hour, and he still hadn't called. Why not?

Or did I already know why not?

Aunt Vivian, passing through the hallway on one of her endless trips to the upstairs bathroom, spotted me slumped in the chair, gazing forlornly at my socks. "Good heavens, Betsy," she asked, "are you still here?" She pursed her lips and gave a knowing look. "If that boy hasn't called by now, he probably never will."

I glanced up, startled. Where had she heard about Rob?

"When a girl sits next to the phone for hours on end and mopes around like a sick calf, you can bet it's because of some boy." She nodded her head as if agreeing with herself.

If wishing could do it, Uncle Frank's wife would be miles away. For one thing, it hadn't been "hours on end." For another, the last person I wanted to hear the truth from was Aunt Vivian.

"I'd give that young man"—she scrutinized her wristwatch—"five more minutes. And then I'd stop thinking about him. Furthermore—"

Cut dead by the jangle of the phone.

Every molecule of me knew it had to be Rob. "Hey, Betsy—" he started.

I directed a stare at Aunt Vivian, who was obviously primed for listening. She backed away reluctantly. "Yes?" I said into the receiver.

"Are you able to talk?"

"Well—" I watched Aunt Vivian eye the bathroom door. "In a minute. I think." She sighed and moved forward. "The coast is clear," I said.

"Betsy, about the story line. I—"

The cousins, all three of them, thundered up the steps, then gathered at the top of the landing where they grappled with one another in a fight to the death.

Aunt Vivian, who's so filled with proper advice for the rest of us, stayed behind the bathroom door, conveniently removing herself from the gang she called her own. It certainly did make a person wonder.

"*Rob*," I shouted above the din, "I'm so sorry—the noise—"

There was sort of a lull in the cousins' battle, during which Rob squeezed in, "We've got to talk, obviously. Where?" And I yelled over the noise that had started up again, "I'll meet you at nine, at the corner of Locust and Pine." Then it all broke loose again. I could only hope Rob had caught what I'd said.

It wasn't all that easy to get away. And, of course, Aunt Vivian didn't exactly help.

"What?" she said, looking scandalized. "You're letting that girl walk downtown—in the dark—alone?" She propped her loafer-clad feet on Dad's hassock and shook her head at Mom. "Grace, sometimes I wonder what you use for common sense."

Mom smiled faintly, counted some sweater stitches under her breath, and continued her knitting.

"I'll tell you one thing, Grace, if *I* had a teen-age daughter, she wouldn't be allowed to—"

"Vivian!" Mom dropped the knitting and turned to stare at Aunt Vivian. Her eyes were glinting the way they do when she's had it. "Will you kindly mind your own business?"

"Well! I must say—"

"Please don't. And let's get the facts straight. Betsy will be walking to the corner of Locust Avenue at nine o'clock to meet Rob Carney, a boy whom I trust completely. They will go downtown—to a perfectly respectable place—where they will eat and talk and have a little innocent fun. He will bring her home before ten-thirty—" Her gaze shifted to me. One brow arched delicately. "Isn't that right, Betsy?"

I nodded.

"I believe," Mom said, "I have made my point." She returned her stare to a spot above the hassock. "Isn't that right, Vivian?"

A pulsating silence from over there.

Except for the noise of the TV and the muffled upstairs sounds of the boys, I could hear only the click of my mother's knitting needles as I hurried into my winter coat and wrapped a scarf around my neck.

I'd slipped on my fur-lined boots, grabbed a pair of mittens, and was heading for the front door when Dad's voice boomed from the other room: "Vivian, how about getting your shoes off the hassock?"

This was followed by the groan of chair springs, which meant Aunt Vivian had hopped to her feet, and the clack-clack of her loafer heels as she left the room in a huff.

I closed the door behind me, not bothering to hide my smile.

Rob was there under the streetlight, glancing anxiously about, when I arrived. "At last," he said, letting out a frosty breath. "I was just starting to think you'd changed your mind." He consulted his digital watch. "You're almost ten minutes late, know that? I've been here since eight forty-seven, and my toes are turning into icicles."

He'd come extra-early and had risked

freezing. For me. "My hero," I said softly. Too softly I thought, for Rob to catch.

His blue-tinged lips parted, forming a grin. "Thanks," he said. "I like you, too."

We walked briskly along, heading for downtown and some reasonably quiet place, preferably one occupied by a few scattered strangers who wouldn't table-hop or interrupt.

What with the holiday weekend, and all, not that much was available to kids our age.

I pressed my face against the plate glass window of BurgerMaster, just in case. "Half the school must be in there," I said. Any other time I'd have jumped at the chance to go in. It was almost like a home away from home.

"Sometimes," Rob said, sliding back from the window, "the best way to be alone is to surround yourself with people."

"Oh, sure."

"Didn't buy that one, huh? Well, try this. There is a certain table, just off the kitchen, where hardly anybody sits. Mostly just the gang who work here. I happen to know a couple of the guys—they're into cartoons—"

"Any reasonable spot, at this point!" I pulled my collar closer about my ears and exhaled a cloud of mist. "It's absolutely freezing out here."

We shoved open the door, dutifully waved to classmates and smiled at friends, and kept gliding forward. I stood by while Rob said a few words to his friends in the kitchen. And finally we had our table—away from all the sights, and most of the sounds, but agreeably close to those delectable kitchen aromas.

Rob ordered cheeseburgers and fries for both of us, plus mugs of steamy hot chocolate. The food did wonders for my empty stomach—I'd been much too nervous at dinner to do more than pick.

The silence between us was the companionable kind, with exploratory smiles exchanged, and eyes catching and holding over the chocolate mugs.

Halfway through the fries, Rob stopped eating. "About you and me," he said. Then he cleared his throat.

I waited for the rest of it. I mean, there *had* to be more.

"What can I say?" He picked at an initial carved into the table top. "You know how it's been. I'd never kept my feelings a secret. From second grade on, you were—the one for me.

162

The only one for me. And then when we got matched up for the cartooning team, it was almost like somebody out there had heard me at last and said, 'Here's your chance, Carney.' But—"

But. What a big word that little word could be.

"That same somebody had forgotten to clue you in."

Not really, Rob. Not really.

Rob took a deep breath. "Anyway, I hadn't planned on my life improving in so many other ways all at once. Carney, the guy no one paid much attention to, suddenly becoming Carney, the cartoonist. First time in my whole life I'd been accepted as being really good at something. And then—when all those girls got interested in me—

"Yeah, things sure are looking up for me," he said. "Popularity—new friends—maybe even a chance to get a head start on my cartooning career." His eyes connected with mine. "Everything your typical guy might want. Right?"

I hesitated. Then, "If you say so, Rob."

"I don't. No way. I'm not your typical guy. So what if things are looking up, things are going my way for a change? I'm like a needle still stuck in the same old groove." He looked at me intently. "When Vicki and Rosemary and everybody started paying all that attention to me, I kind of got sidetracked, carried away by all the fuss. But now that I'm getting used to it, I realize that I still want what I wanted from the beginning. The right girl for me. And the right girl has to be you."

I opened my mouth, smartened up, closed my mouth.

"So, I cooked up this great scheme, see? Even hired my sister to play a fat role in it. No problem there, since she already thinks she's star material. OK, so I inked and tinted this sketch of you, dressed it like Rosalie, then oh-so-casually slid it into the folder and sent it home with you. I hoped you'd see it, understand, and give me a chance this time. It was a gamble. I mean, the way you *usually* overreact. . . . Well, anyway, I went through the motions of living for the next couple of hours. And then—"

"And then," I put it neatly, "you got my new story."

A moment, suspended in space, during which Rob examined his knuckles and I concentrated on a cobweb along the ceiling.

When we broke the silence, our voices jumbled together. I let mine trail away, to allow Rob's baritone some breathing space. He spoke for both of us when he said simply, "We make a terrific team." And then he broke into that fabulous smile—just for me.

The walk back home took time. Especially since Rob and I were in no hurry to get away from each other, even for a few hours.

I was amazed at how much we had to talk about. It was as if we'd kept hidden tons of unspoken words that we'd been saving for a special occasion. And the special occasion had finally arrived.

We discussed, among other things, the National Young Cartoonist contest. Rob was pretty confident. "We've got an excellent chance, Betsy. Mr. Baldwin's real proud of 'Windy.' And he's up on all that contest stuff."

"It's terribly important to you that we win, isn't it?" I could see that in his face. "OK, if it's all that important to you, it's all that important to me."

We slowed down as we neared Locust Avenue. Rob removed my mittens and warmed my hands in his. "Of course, it's important," he said. "Can't you guess why?"

I could think of many reasons.

"Because of us, dummy!" His grip on my fingers tightened. "OK, I'll spell it out. It's like the Walpoles were tiny sparks somewhere inside our heads, just waiting to be found. And then one day you and I got out the sketch pad and the thinking cap, and these people—Windy, Hannah, and Rosalie—all of a sudden caught fire and blew to life. You and I did that. We created characters. *Our* characters. I consider that important, Betsy." Rob put his face close to mine. "Don't you?"

I liked the way the boy's mind worked.

Furthermore, I liked the coziness of the inside of his jacket pocket, where he'd tucked my bare left hand, and covered it with his own. I even liked his off-key rendition of that dreamy song we'd danced to at the Harvest Ball. It added to the spirit of our trek home.

We paused under the streetlight in front of my house to try out a couple of dance steps; then we stopped and stood together, with his arm loosely resting on my shoulder.

"Want to come in for some popcorn and a late night movie on TV?"

"Boy, *would* I!"

Still Rob's arm stayed where it was, only tighter, hugging me to him. I was in no mood to argue with that.

After a while it seemed sensible to nudge him just a little with "I suppose we should go in—"

"Betsy—?"

I caught the huskiness in his voice. And I didn't need ESP to know what was coming. It had to be the most natural thing in the world for me to turn my face to meet his.

Rob Carney, it would seem, is a guy of many talents. And someday I may tell him what his kiss did to my nervous system. If, that is, he tells me first where he learned how to do it with such finesse.

But time enough later for questions and answers. As of that moment, in that particular place, I did something else that came naturally. I grabbed my guy by the elbow, propelled him up the front walk, and hustled him into the warmth and light of the Marsh family living room.

Rob and I were out of the cold for good.

**Watch for Something Special
Coming from Sweet Dreams
in January 1985**

STAR STRUCK!

by
Shannon Blair

It's the thrill of a lifetime when Carrie is cast as an extra in a rock video starring Michael Jackson! The work is a dream come true—there's even a romance with Joe, another extra. Things seem to be going great for Carrie, until her expectations get a little out of hand . . .

Buy STAR STRUCK! on sale January 15, 1985 wherever Bantam paperbacks are sold.

You'll fall in love with all the Sweet Dream romances. Reading these stories, you'll be reminded of yourself or of someone you know. There's Jennie, the *California Girl*, who becomes an outsider when her family moves to Texas. And Cindy, the *Little Sister*, who's afraid that Christine, the oldest in the family, will steal her new boyfriend. Don't miss any of the Sweet Dreams romances.

☐ 24460	P.S. I LOVE YOU #1 Barbara P. Conklin	$2.25
☐ 24332	THE POPULARITY PLAN #2 Rosemary Vernon	$2.25
☐ 24318	LAURIE'S SONG #3 Debra Brand	$2.25
☐ 14020	PRINCESS AMY #4 Melinda Pollowitz	$1.95
☐ 24319	LITTLE SISTER #5 Yvonne Green	$2.25
☐ 24320	CALIFORNIA GIRL #6 Janet Quin-Harkin	$2.25
☐ 14022	GREEN EYES #7 Suzanne Rand	$1.95
☐ 24322	THE THOROUGHBRED #8 Joanna Campbell	$2.25
☐ 24323	COVER GIRL #9 Yvonne Green	$2.25
☐ 24324	LOVE MATCH #10 Janet Quin-Harkin	$2.25
☐ 24312	THE PROBLEM WITH LOVE #11 Rosemary Vernon	$2.25
☐ 24832	NIGHT OF THE PROM #12 Debra Spector	$2.25
☐ 24333	THE SUMMER JENNY FELL IN LOVE #13 Barbara Conklin	$2.25
☐ 24290	DANCE OF LOVE #14 Jocelyn Saal	$2.25
☐ 24742	THINKING OF YOU #15 Jeanette Nobile	$2.25
☐ 24315	HOW DO YOU SAY GOODBYE #16 Margaret Burman	$2.25
☐ 24326	ASK ANNIE #17 Suzanne Rand	$2.25
☐ 24291	TEN-BOY SUMMER #18 Janet Quin-Harkin	$2.25
☐ 22542	LOVE SONG #19 Anne Park	$1.95
☐ 24466	THE POPULARITY SUMMER #20 Rosemary Vernon	$2.25
☐ 22607	ALL'S FAIR IN LOVE #21 Jeanne Andrews	$1.95

☐ 24327	SECRET IDENTITY #22	$2.25
	Joanna Campbell	
☐ 24407	FALLING IN LOVE AGAIN #23	$2.25
	Barbara Conklin	
☐ 24329	THE TROUBLE WITH CHARLIE #24	$2.25
	Jaye Ellen	
☐ 22543	HER SECRET SELF #25	$1.95
	Rhondi Villot	
☐ 24292	IT MUST BE MAGIC #26	$2.25
	Marian Woodruff	
☐ 22681	TOO YOUNG FOR LOVE #27	$1.95
	Gailanne Maravel	
☐ 23053	TRUSTING HEARTS #28	$1.95
	Jocelyn Saal	
☐ 24312	NEVER LOVE A COWBOY #29	$2.25
	Jesse Dukore	
☐ 24293	LITTLE WHITE LIES #30	$2.25
	Lois I. Fisher	
☐ 23189	TOO CLOSE FOR COMFORT #31	$1.95
	Debra Spector	
☐ 24837	DAY DREAMER #32	$2.25
	Janet Quin-Harkin	
☐ 23283	DEAR AMANDA #33	$1.95
	Rosemary Vernon	
☐ 23287	COUNTRY GIRL #34	$1.95
	Melinda Pollowitz	
☐ 24336	FORBIDDEN LOVE #35	$2.25
	Marian Woodruff	
☐ 24338	SUMMER DREAMS #36	$2.25
	Barbara Conklin	
☐ 23340	PORTRAIT OF LOVE #37	$1.95
	Jeanette Noble	
☐ 24331	RUNNING MATES #38	$2.25
	Jocelyn Saal	
☐ 24340	FIRST LOVE #39	$2.25
	Debra Spector	
☐ 24315	SECRETS #40	$2.25
	Anna Aaron	
☐ 24838	THE TRUTH ABOUT ME AND BOBBY V. #41	$2.25
	Janetta Johns	
☐ 23532	THE PERFECT MATCH #42	$1.95
	Marian Woodruff	
☐ 23533	TENDER-LOVING-CARE #43	$1.95
	Anne Park	
☐ 23534	LONG DISTANCE LOVE #44	$1.95
	Jesse Dukore	
☐ 24341	DREAM PROM #45	$2.25
	Margaret Burman	
☐ 23697	ON THIN ICE #46	$1.95
	Jocelyn Saal	
☐ 23743	TE AMO MEANS I LOVE YOU #47	$1.95
	Deborah Kent	

Prices and availability subject to change without notice.